EFFECTIVE IMMEDIATELY

BY

Gail Anderson

B.gl🦁bal Publishing

Effective Immediately

Edited by Christina M. Long, CML Collective, LLC
Cover and interior design by Christina M. Long
Although every effort has been made to ensure the accuracy and completeness of the information contained in this book, the producer, publisher and printer disclaim any personal liability, either directly or indirectly, for any infringement of copyright or otherwise arising from the contents of this publication

First edition printed: 2015

Printed in the United States

~Acknowledgements~

I would like to give thanks to my Lord and Savior for giving me the knowledge, strength and determination to overcome adversities in life and helping me prevail over each of them.

To my mother Sharon Flowers: There are not enough words to give thanks to you. You have been a pillar of strength, a best friend to me, and a shoulder to cry on when in need. Mom, I love you not just for being my mother, but also for being the Matriarch of our family, and loving me in a manner that only a mother can. Thank you mommy!

To my daddy, Richard Boswell: You are such a wonderful dad, the best a daughter could ask for. You've stepped up to the plate, raising me since I was 16 months. I could not ask for a better dad. I love you with all my heart, and am forever grateful and will always be your "Nut Bucket"!

My sister Shawn: I must say you keep things interesting and stay on top of your game. I know that when it comes down to it, you are there for me and have my back no matter what. For the longest you, mom and I were the "three amigos" and will always have that special and unbreakable bond. Stay focused "lil big sis." I love you always.

To my niece Sharon, aka "Shae": You are a wonderful young woman who has a fabulous sense of style and personality. It seems surreal how quickly you've grown from a cute and cuddly toddler to such an intelligent and beautiful young lady. Auntie is so proud of you. Love you, Puggly!

To Anthony: You are a Godsend to my family. Thank you for helping with the care of my mom, Sharon Flowers, who loves only your coffee by the way, lol. I wish you well, on whatever path you choose, with this thing we call life. Remember, life is not a dress rehearsal so live it to the fullest. God Bless!

~Dedications~

Zephyr Lee Elizabeth Rollie, my loving grandmother, your name means "like the wind or gently breeze. So is your kindred spirit. I love you so much grandma. I admired you for your wisdom, words of encouragement, and faith you had in the Lord. It is a joy and gives me pride to have been your granddaughter. I am blessed to have had you as a part of my life for many years, as well. Rest in loving paradise. You will be remembered always.

To Lonnie Frank Reed, my father. Dad, you are sorely missed. There is not a day that goes by that I don't think of you. You were tragically taken from me way too soon. When you left this earth, a part of me slipped away. This year, I was looking at Father's Day cards, when I began to cry. Suddenly, I felt a soft touch on my shoulder and turned around. No one was there, but I knew it was you telling me it will be all right. So, as life goes on, I will carry out the Reed legacy and cherish memories well spent. I love you dad; gone but never forgotten!

PRELUDE
4 in the morning!

'Lord, Jesus why? Please tell me that is not the phone I hear. I pray that whoever sits on the other end better be bloody or about to knock on Heaven's door! It would be nice, if I could open my eyes, to lock in on the target who has broken my rest.'

I managed to open my eyelids, which both felt like somebody crazy glued while I was sleeping and clumsily grab the phone.

"Hello," I whispered.

No answer.

I cleared my throat to rid the dryness of my tongue, hoping that the words would stronger and clearer.

"I need to speak with Myles," the person on the other end of the phone said, with much attitude.

'Help me NOW, Jesus!' I begged gripping my covers to avoid going off on a disrespectful heffa who I knew all too well.

First of all, she had no manners. She didn't say, "May I speak to Myles, kiss my ass, or how you doing Brooke?"

I hesitated for a moment then reached over and nudged my husband to tell him his *ex-wife*— aka baby's momma — was on the phone.

"Huh?" he mumbled through sleep.

"Tashia is on the phone," I told him with plenty of irritation to help convey my feelings regarding this situation.

"I'm tired,woman," he whined, "and who is it, anyways?"

Getting even more pissed off, I placed my knee into his back and yelled, "HANDLE IT! GET THAT CHICK IN PLACE!"

Myles chucked the questions, manned up and grabbed the phone from my hand.

"What Tashia?"

As Myles continued to talk to his *ex- NUT*, I couldn't help but to reflect about how this heffa had some nerve calling my house, disrespecting me, and demanding to speak to my husband. Let's not forget that it was three hours before the sun was set to dawn. I was just starting to get my deep sleep on around that time. The trick had all the nerves of brave.

Watching and listening closely, Myles sat up in the bed and breathed a heavy sigh.

"What is it, Tashia?"

"I called to clear the air about the argument we had the other day," I could hear her say.

"This conversation couldn't wait till a decent time of the day?" Myles asked furiously, while taking notes about the precious moments of sleep he was missing.

"I was up rolling my hair and, suddenly, God told me to call and clear the air," she said.

'Okay this chick is crazy. Someone process the psycho checks, please!' I couldn't help but think.

From the moment Tashia knew that Myles had moved on and had a new woman in his life, she made it her goal to be a rotten sore in his side. In her world, I was always known as his "little girlfriend." If anything, I was their daughters' "real mother." Any woman could have a child, but a real woman raises that child to be righteous and to know right from wrong.

Talk about being ungrateful.

I remember the time when Myles and I purchased and mailed off his two girls a box full of clothes. Once Tashia received the clothes in the mail, complaints — instead of thanks— flew from that trap mouth of hers. I hated how the baby mamas play those childish games on women who have probably done it— or saw it done — at some point in their lives. Complaints ranged from, "The clothes are going to shrink once I wash them" to "These outfits look like something your little girlfriend picked out" and "For real, no brand-name clothes? What type of foolishness is this?"

Finally, at the end of their conversation, she would mumble a, "Thank you."

It was always something with that woman.

I was ready to tell Myles, "Forget it. Just do child support. Let the courts decide and then that's it!"

I hated to be like that because no child should be brought up that way, but, sometimes....mess just flows down before it hits the fan.

It was nothing for her to make demands, though, saying: "The kids need this, the girls needed money for some event at school, and they need money for their extra-curricular activities."

Did the woman not know the meaning of extra?

I felt that Tashia knew that she could call and dismiss me as his lady because she had something I did not have with my husband —children.

This has to stop and I'm going to be the one to put an end to it for once and for all,' I thought.

Later on that day, I called Tashia, who lived with her aunt in a tiny row home in Brooklyn. On the second ring, her aunt Sybil answered the phone.

"Hello Sybil. May I speak with Tashia?" I held the phone away from my ear to keep my eardrum intact from her aunt shouting so loudly that it could have awakened a dead man.

It didn't take long before I heard another phone line being picked up.

"Hello Tashia. This is Brooke," I said.

She didn't respond so I repeated myself. "I'm here!" she snapped back.

I had made myself a promise not to cop an attitude with Ms. Thang and so I kept my cool while I explained, "I don't feel what you did this morning was appropriate. I mean, four A.M.? You thought that you and him would be in your right minds, at that time in the morning, to resolve and settle whatever y'all got going on?"

That statement too, was also met with silence. By that time I was doing the Angela Bassett thing in *"What's Love Got to do With It."* My thumbs touching my pointer finger, eyes closed, quietly under the palate of my tongue, I peacefully chanted away, *'nam-myoho-renge-kyo.'* I did that three times.

"Did you hear what I said?" I questioned again.

"I heard you but if something is wrong or if the girls are sick, I'm going to call."

The meditation didn't help. It was on.

"If you call at four in the morning one more time, you will hear a message saying, 'The number you have dialed is not accepting calls from this party. If you feel this is an error, dial again or check with the operator!' On that note, enjoy talking to the operator in five, four, three, two, and one!" I said as I slammed the phone down. I'm sure my wrist was sprained by the way I slammed the phone down.

'Lord I am really trying to deal with all this drama, but there's no pleasing this woman. She uses the girls to get whatever she wants out of Myles, and knows he'll go over and beyond for his babies,' I prayed.

Little did Tashia know that her lies, deceptions, and the use of the children as pawns were going to be her downfall in a couple of years to come.

Chapter One
Ice Storm

There wasn't much to do, so I tuned in to my good old house Doctor. I was in the middle of watching Dr. Phil, shaking my head in pure disbelief over the fact that a woman on the show would allow her teenage children to purchase and watch porn. Dr. Phil confronted her about it and she was in complete denial.

'Sista girl is going to burn for that one.'

It was the middle of winter and I was freezing even though the heat was a blaring eighty degrees. It sounded as if huge rocks were beating against the roof of my house. The weather forecaster predicted that the area in which I resided would be under a winter weather warning for the next six to eight hours. It was raining baseball-sized hail and, by the time that the rain would reach the ground, it would freeze over. I could hear the tree branches crackle and fall to the ground from the heavy weight of the ice that was freezing upon them. Since the ground was completely covered with frozen ice, the sound of the tree branches hitting the ground echoed throughout the neighborhood.

In the middle of Dr. Phil confronting the porn mother, my power went out.

"Dagnabbit! Well I guess I gotta see you later, Dr. Phil."

I got up to look out my back window. What I saw made my mouth drop to the floor. A huge tree that had to be at least fifty years old had fallen on the transformer that generated electricity to neighborhoods for several blocks. Sparks were popping while a few wires were moving like snakes twisting among one another.

Still shaking my head in disbelief, I grabbed my cell phone from the charger and stomped back into my bedroom. I dialed the seven digits to the power company and followed the one hundred prompts it took to reach a customer service agent. I hated those prompts.

"Press one for English. Press two to change your service. Press three if you get sick of pressing buttons and want to talk to a real person."

I would have done better dialing 911. After holding for what seemed like an eternity, an agent came on the line — or so I thought. The voice recording stated that due to a high volume of calls, my wait time would be over an hour.

'*Wait over an hour?*' I complained to myself. I'd be a popsicle by then. The automated voice said that I could press nine to report a power outage. I almost broke a nail trying to jab at the buttons on the phone like it was going to help. All I could do was wait and hope that the power company would be out soon to restore power so I could catch *"Girlfriends"* by eight o'clock.

I put on an extra pair of socks and my Bugs Bunny slippers, and then wrapped myself in my favorite comforter. I was trying to stay warm and keep my mind off the fact that the house was getting colder by the hour. Sleep began resting heavily upon my eyelids.

I must have dozed off because I awakened to the sound of more tree branches hitting the house and the ground outside and my cell phone reading nine p.m. I didn't realize that I had slept for so long. I grabbed the television remote and pressed the power button on and nothing came to. I couldn't believe that the power company hadn't been out to restore services.

I called my mom to see if she had any power. She answered after the third ring. "Hey mom-has your power gone out?"

"No," she said, "but they did flicker for a few seconds about three hours ago."

"Well mine went out around three-thirty and I'm still in the dark."

"Do you want to come over here?" she asked. "You know I have plenty of room."

"Nah, I'll try to stick it out here until my power comes back on. I don't want to risk it with the road conditions. I know the streets are slippery and are covered with ice."

"Ok honey, but you know that you can always come here and keep warm."

"Yes I know and thanks for the offer," I said. "I'll call you when the power comes back on in a couple of hours."

I'm so glad that I wasn't holding my breath until the power came back on because it took 10 days to restore.

I ended up staying at my mother's house, after all. Officials had closed down schools, local, city and federal buildings due to the ice storm. People around the city had no way of keeping warm due to lack of power and were forced to seek shelter at school gyms that were turned into temporary housing. I was also out of work for a week at the law firm I worked for. With nothing to do but ride out the bad weather, I grabbed my journal of poetry and began to write.

I was so deep in my words that I didn't hear my cell phone ring. When I reviewed my missed calls, one number sent me into a rage causing me to grit and grind my teeth.

'Damn, damn, damn. How did he get my cell phone number?' I was so done with him. In fact, and he was the reason why I changed my number in the first place.

Jonathan was my ex-husband who would not leave me alone despite the restraining order I had against him. During our marriage, Jonathan and I had a love/hate relationship— I loved to hate him. He considered himself to be a lady's man even during our marriage. With his drinking, drug use and staying out all night, I got fed up with his *"Baby, I'm sorry. It won't happen again."* The way he sang that lame song so much, you would have thought it made Billboard's top ten list.

'Umm hmm. Save that line for someone who gives a damn playa.' So after ten long years of marriage, I dumped him like the trash he was. I filed for divorce and kicked his no-good, arrogant "Taye Diggs wannabe-looking behind out. Now one of his dingy chicks could take care of him and put up with his foolish ways.

'They don't have to be the secret lady no more. They can have him as well as become the one who gets cheated on! That entire ruckus and boatload of arguments just to get cheated on? So not worth it,' was my soapbox I pulled out over and over again when it came to him. So when I saw his number show up on my cell phone, I sent him to voicemail. Several seconds later, the message ringtone jingled. I deleted that one along with the many others he had left. Jonathan called several times after that. Finally, after being sick and tired of being sick and tired of him calling me back-to-back, I answered.

"Hey pretty lady," he sang. "Why have you been avoiding me?"

Turns out, he was drunk.

"What is it that you want, Jonathan? I don't have time for the bull crap so get straight to the point."

"Aww sugar baby, is that any way to treat your first love? I just wanted to see how you were and make sure that you are okay," He said, "I'm fine, not that it's any of your business. Do you know that you're violating the restraining order?"

"Girl, you know that no piece of paper can keep me away from your fine self. I still remember those pretty full lips of yours and those thick juicy thighs. They still belong to me, remember? I have your name tattooed on my chest! That means forever!" he said more aggressively.

"What brand of crack have you been smoking? Is it the one that makes you dumb or the one that makes you hallucinate that there would be a snowball's chance inside the gates of hell which would make me take you back?" I exclaimed.

I heard him chuckle at that comment and then things took a drastic change.

"Let me tell you something, Brooke: no matter what, or whom you see, screw or marry, you'll always be mine! No divorce papers, no restraining order or the law can keep me away from you. You're my property and I want what's mine."

"Jonathan, take a long walk from the shortest pier," I boldly said. "You're getting on the only nerve that I have left, and if you think that you can run me and look at me as a piece of property, you got another thing coming. I will hurt you in ways that would make you hate me for life.

"Keep threatening *me* if you want to, Jonathan. I promise you will regret it!"

Something inside that empty and dumb head of his switched, and his whole attitude changed.

"Now sugar lump, I didn't mean any harm. I'm sorry if I offended you baby, you know I was just playing," he said.

"Whatever Jonathan. Believe me when I tell you that I don't play when it comes to you making idle threats."

"All right all right," he said chuckling. "The last thing that I wanted to do was to make you mad. I just miss you and I wanted to see you if you would let me take you to dinner."

By this time, I was gritting my teeth out of frustration.

"Look I gotta go, I have another call," I lied.

"Wait a second, sugar cube."

Click.

I pushed the "end" button and stared at my phone.

17 • Effective Immediately

*'What the hell is up with the sugar reference?' I thought.
'Do I look like a piece of sugar cane to him? After being
called sugar so many times, I got a cavity. When will he get
the hint?'*

The nut had messed up my vibe. I wouldn't finish any
more writing that night so I turned my attention outside,
watching all the cars pass by the front window to unknown
destinations.

Chapter Two
There's No Place Like Home

As I re-entered my home for the first time after the storm, I realized that it was cooler inside than outside. It didn't even faze me, though. I was so happy to have power that all else didn't matter. Plus, I could heat the house in a good hour. I took my gloves off to adjust the thermostat to heat things up. Then, I went to the kitchen and bathrooms to check the water pipes. With it being so cold outside I thought they would have either busted or froze over.

'*Yes!*' I snapped my fingers. There were no busted pipes. If it happened again, I made a note to remember to le the water drain run low. I knew that the food in the fridge was spoiled so I had stopped by the grocery store and stocked up on groceries. I cleaned my refrigerator out with bleach and hot water because I was old school like that I also started putting the last of the groceries away when my phone rang.

"Hello," I said with a mouth full of an ice cream snack.

"Hey girl, it's about time your raggedy behind came home," my best friend, Gabrielle, chimed in.

Gabby was my nickname for her since middle school. She was a tall, shapely, mocha- colored sister. She had wild, frizzy hair that was the color of straw honey attributed to her biracial heritage. Her mom was from Ghana and her pops was Portuguese. She had almond-shaped green eyes that could stop traffic for days.

Gabby had a lot of issues growing up because she was taller than most kids our age and lanky, at best. Since her mom bailed out on her and her three other siblings, Gabby's dad had to provide for the family and work several odd jobs to keep food on the table. It was hard for Gabby growing up being the oldest and living in the projects. Wrapped around her neck, like a scarf, was prostitution, murders and drug transactions happening at all times during the day and night that Gabby tried hard to suppress.

She rarely talked about events of her past. She made the best of her environment and was determined to make something of her life rather than being another statistic. She was trying to get out of the projects — alive.

The summer before we both were to enter high school, Gabby developed overnight. The tall skinny girl sprung so many curves it should have been a traffic violation. She took control of her unruly mane and turned it into manageable ringlets. A rich, young twenty-something-year-old heiress, who Gabby's father did lawn work for three times a week, knew that he was a struggling father of four. She changed her wardrobe every season and donated last season's clothes to charity. One afternoon while Gabby's dad finished planting flowers, the heiress told him that she had several boxes full of clothes for him to take home to his girls.

She told him that she didn't want to offend, just help him. The woman went on to state how Gabby's dad was so good to her and her family throughout all his years of service. He told her that she had done more than enough since his pay was always over the amount that he charged.

"Please take them, I'd rather give them to you and I know it will help you out! Most men in your situation would have given up, but you stayed and have been the best father that you can be. I admire you for that and wished I'd had a father like you," Gabby would tell me that her father shared with her.

He arrived home with boxes loaded up in his truck and had his son take them into the apartment. Gabby and the rest of the girls went through the box as if it was Christmas in July. Gabby and her twin sisters were each about the same size. Each girl managed to find enough outfits to last them for weeks without having to wear the same thing twice. Gabby arrived on the first day school like she had just stepped off the runway. Tyra Banks would have had to look twice and straighten her catwalk up! I did a flashback to that time remembering how I did a double take and mumbled "Gabby?"

"What's up missy?" Gabby said. "How are things poppin' in your world?" She quizzed as she spun around. After managing to pick my jaw up from the ground, I told her that she looked fly.

"I love those shoes that you're rockin'," I remembered saying. "Go on Miss Thang!"

I would never forget how we both passed by the uppity crew and started laughing hysterically when we saw the "Who done it and what for?" look on their faces. It was a priceless moment that we both still talked about.

Turning my attention back to our phone conversation, I said, "same to you heffa!" with my hands on my hips as I smacked in her ear. "Girl it's good to be back home in my own crib. Don't get me wrong; I'm thankful that mom's offered me a place to stay. You know what Dorothy said? 'There's no place like home,'" I said while clicking my heels three times just to give the saying some meaning.

We both laughed.

I laughed even harder while Gabby did her impression of the Cowardly Lion.

"Put 'em up, put 'em up.

"Girl, you know you need to quit!" I laughed, while dropping some of my ice cream on the floor. "Whew, my side hurts from laughing so hard. Thanks for the laugh girl!

"So what's on your agenda for tonight?" Gabby asked.

"Nothing much," I said. "Might catch up on some laundry and check my email. I probably have a couple of hundred emails —most of them junk mail to delete. What are you up to this evening?" I asked.

"I plan on checking out this new jazz joint on 18th and Vine called the Blue Room. I hear it's the hot spot for the mature adults and the cover charge and drinks don't cost an arm and a leg," she said.

"Are you going solo or taking that fine, bald black brotha you've been dating?"

"Didn't I tell you: I found out that he was married, two kids with one on the way *and* unemployed while he was living in his momma's basement?"

"Dang, for real it's like that," I asked.

"No, it *was* like that! I call blocked his lazy behind and told his wifey all about his bull."

Gabby ran on as if time was forever.

"Girl, you've got more drama than a soap opera and a Broadway play put together. You need to slow your roll and be selective about these funny-looking, fake men out there."

"I know I know.... but the loving was good. He had a girl's toes curling and had me singing his name like Destiny's Child sung in their heydays," she said.

That comment started a whole new round of side-splitting laughs.

"I don't have time for you girly," I said. "I'm about to order Chinese delivery, put on some Will Downing and take a long hot bath."

"Go do your thing and I will hit you back later on sometime in the week, Brooke."

"Alrighty then, Gabby. Enjoy your evening and let me know how you like the new jazz joint.

"Chat with you later," we both said in unison. I smiled to myself, "That's my girl!"

Chapter Three
The Email

My boy Will Downing was belting out silky smooth vocals on my CD player. They should've outlawed sounding as sexy as that bald, dark specimen. He was singing about taking the day off from work and chilling with his girl.

"Lucky ass chick." I said aloud.

I stepped from the shower and grabbed my favorite fluffy towel and dried off. Steam blurred the bathroom mirror so I wiped it off with my hand and peered into it to study my face from side to side. No gray hairs or wrinkles, yet. After seeing a dermatologist about the acne I had, my skin was as smooth as whipped cream. I continued to dry off.

Once I was all dry, I released my shoulder-length hair from the clip that I used to keep it from getting wet. I put cucumber melon-scented lotion on my slightly damp skin and then sprayed on a little shower and bath spritz. I loved the smell of cucumber melon. I made sure to visit Bath and Body Works every few months. After putting on my purple lounger and my bunny slippers, I grabbed my food, chopsticks and my favorite wine cooler, Fuzzy Navel, and headed for my bedroom. I got comfortable on my queen-sized bed with fluffy pillows surrounding me and began to chow down. My laptop sat beside me and, after a few bites of shrimp fried rice, I turned on my laptop to get caught up on my emails. Three hundred and forty-six new emails were waiting for me to delete in my bulk mail.

"Okay, I'll clear those out."

After that, I checked my inbox. There were twenty-two new messages. Many of them were from Gabby, who sent them while she was at work. Several of them were from my online chat buddies who sent me different messages ranging from how to get rich or just checking to see how I survived the ice storm.

I'd read most of the emails — at least the ones that mattered to me—yet I came to one that caught my eye. The title of it was a simple, "Hello" but that wasn't what held my attention. The username was "Compozer." I was curious and wanted to see who this Compozer was since I didn't have any friends by that name.

I opened the email and saw that he had left a simple paragraph that read, "I just stopped by your neck of the woods to say hello and to compliment you on how beautiful you are. You have a glow that piques all my manly interests. I like your vibe.

I enjoy reading the poetry that you have on your page. I would like to read more if you would allow me to. I also look forward to hearing from you. And, by the way, *love those lips.*" I looked at the date and time and saw that Compozer had sent it five days ago. It was the only one that he had sent. By that time I was thinking to myself and wondering if I should reply back.

'What if he is some Internet stalker or some horny dude looking for cyber sex? If he fits into any one of those boats, then he can float on! I'm not the one.'

Finally, zipping through the messages to make sure I read them all, I checked my last email. I was ready to log off and continue munching when my eyes gazed back to the email that Compozer sent me.

"Oh, what can it hurt?"

'Girl, ain't any harm in saying hello and thanks for dropping by. That's my usual response to folks who browse my page to leave a note, anyways.'

After typing the short message, I logged off and continued eating the remainder of my food. I started my DVD player and watched my favorite, "Imitation of Life" movie. The wine cooler placed me in a mellow mood and, before long, I was nodding off. Determined not to fall face-first in my food, I put my food container aside on my nightstand and slid underneath the warmth of my comforter. I set my alarm on my cell phone for five a.m. and rolled over to a comfortable position.

After several minutes, I fell into a dreamless slumber.

Chapter Four
The Response

My feet were barking. I called myself trying to look cute by wearing my *'time limit'* heels to the mall —you know, those special high heels that a woman can only stand to be in for a limited amount of time? I don't know what I was I thinking. With fresh pedicured feet, I dared not to cover them and mess up my fuchsia-colored toes. I untied my sling-backs and placed them back into their rightful storage box.

That night, I wore a black and white wrap dress that I had purchased from Lane Bryant on that day. I looked good, too. I completed my look with small diamond studs and my silver watch on one arm and a set of bangles on the other. Since I was a plus-sized sister, I had to make sure that my style was tight. To do that, I scheduled lots of shopping trips. Hanging with my girl, Gabby, we'd meet up over lunch a few times a month and do some shopping at the malls.

When we'd be together, I could turn just as many heads as Gabby. I was blessed to have a nice, voluptuous shape with a behind that could make a blind man feel my thunder as I passed by — or so I was told. My double-digit dress size has paid off for me in more ways than one. For example, it helped me get a great deal on my SUV. The salesman was this fine, light-skinned brother who had teeth so white, they could light up a room. He worked a deal out for me so good that I was able to walk away with no money down and a reasonable note each month. After the sale completed, the salesman was walking me to my new ride when I, suddenly, turned around to ask him a question and caught him gazing at my rump shaker. I laughed when he began to blush and asked him about the warranty to my new ride. As I was leaving, he handed me his business card and told me that if I had any questions, never hesitate to call him. He took my right hand and kissed it.

'Umph,' he was really kicking it on strong. I had to admit, I was flirting back, but I kept it subtle.

Settling in for the night, I grabbed a pair of sweats and a white tee shirt that had "Diva" printed in rhinestones on it, then put on a cute pair of flip-flops that also had rhinestones on the band of them. My hair, which was wrapped, was easy to manage with my hectic schedule. I grabbed a banana clip and put the back of my hair up. "There, geared for comfort."

I plugged my laptop in to charge since I had taken it to work with me to earlier in the week. I logged on to the Internet and began checking my emails.

"Well look, here," I see that Mr. Compozer had responded to my previous email. I begin reading it aloud.

"Well hello to you. How are you doing today? I hope that this note finds you in good spirits this sunny spring day. I was pleasantly surprised to receive a response from a beautiful woman such as you. It made my day. I don't want to come off too strong and would never want to offend you in any manner. I am a member of a website called, 'Mocha People.' It's an African American website geared to people and issues of color. If you have the time, you can look at my profile and get a better idea of who I am. My username is the same as the one I used on my email to you. Well, take care Ms. Lady and I hope to hear from you soon. Have a splendid afternoon.

Compozer."

I was familiar with Mocha People. I even had a membership. I decide to log onto the website to ease my curiosities. I clicked on the search button and typed in his username. A black screen popped up before my eyes and then, in slow motion, a background evolved. His background was that of a jazz setting. It showed a picture of people sipping on wine while listening to a jazz quartet in the background. One musician was playing the saxophone, the other was on drums. Also, a handsome big and tall brother with a neatly trimmed beard was playing the piano. He toggled the keys with his head tilted to the side and eyes closed. The jazz singer was a woman dressed in a free-flowing, red, knee-length dress.

As I began to read his page, he told how he was a musician who played the saxophone and the piano. He was even pictured on the background playing the piano. So "Compozer" was the handsome caramel-colored man on the piano. I gazed at the picture for several minutes and continued to read the rest of his page. He went on to tell about his interests and what he does in his spare time when not working. His profile stated that he was not looking but was basically on the website to meet new and interesting people. I also noted those tidbits and stored them in the back of my mind.

At the bottom of his page, he placed a full-body picture of himself with a sly smile. I could see that he was dressed nicely and not too flamboyant. He was wearing simple black slacks and a black shirt that opened around the neck. He was wearing a silver watch and a silver pinky ring on one hand. On a scale of one to ten, he would be a ten in my book.

"He's online," I said to myself.

Before I knew it, I had clicked on the page button and typed, "Hello, how are you today? I got your message and wanted to respond back.

"If you would like to chat, you can reach me at my instant messenger, *thickwitit32*, on Yahoo. I look forward to hearing from you. Have a great afternoon."

I thought about deleting the message; I clicked on the send button.

"There!" I said to myself, "It's done."

I didn't know why I was so nervous. You would have thought that I was a blushing, giddy sixteen-year-old hyperactive teenager. Well, I couldn't take it back. The deed was done.

After several minutes, a notification popped up from Compozer. It read that he was happy to hear from me and that he would, most definitely, like to chat with me. With high anticipation, I logged on to Yahoo! and typed in his username. Once the instant messenger window popped open I typed in a simple, "Hello."

Compozer: *"Well hello to you beautiful. How are things going with you today?"*

Thickwitit32: *"Everything is great with me."*

Compozer: *"I'm glad that I am able to chat with you. You have been on my mind. What is on your agenda for today?"*

Thickwitit32:*"Nothing much. I plan on taking easy by the neck and riding that out for the rest of the day. It will probably be a movie night; nothing too exciting. What about you?" I replied.*

Compozer: *"I'm working on some tracks in my studio. I'm trying to put something together for my CD."*

Thickwitit32:*"So you also produce, write and play?"*

Compozer: *"Yes I do. Music is my first love. I get lost in producing for several hours and don't keep track of the time."*

Thickwitit32: *"How long have you been playing the piano and the saxophone?"*

Compozer: *"Since I was a teenager in high school. I originally began playing the saxophone and my interest piqued with the piano. My music instructor wanted me to play the sax, instead, so I had to teach myself how to play the piano, while focusing on the sax lessons."*

'Very interesting,' I thought. 'It makes me wanna learn more. Not only is a brother sexy but he's smart, too!'

We typed each other back and forth for about an hour; chatting as if we were long lost friends who had years to catch up on. It was getting late so I told him that I enjoyed his conversation but I had an early morning so I had to log off soon. He replied by saying that he looked forward to hearing from me again.

Compozer: *"Enjoy your night, Ms. Lady."*

Thickwitit32: *"You do the same. Oh, by the way, what is your real name?"*

Compozer: *"My name is Myles, and what is yours?"*

Thickwitit32: *"Brooke. It's very nice to have chatted with you."*

Compozer: *"It was my pleasure,"* Myles replied. *"I will chat with you soon, beautiful. Good night."*

Thickwitit32: "*I look forward to the same. Good night.*"

What a night. My fingers ached from typing so long and fast. I had a wonderful time chatting with Myles. We were able to chat about our interest, hobbies, likes and dislikes. I saved him to my buddy list and logged off. It was after ten o' clock and my eyes were starting to burn. I changed into my night clothes and slid into bed.

Myles stayed on my mind. I wondered how his voice sounded.

'*Would I be too bold by leaving him my number?*'

I pondered that question until sleep took hold of me.

Chapter Five
The Fender Bender

As I was on my way to work, I turned on the radio to listen to the same old traffic conditions. I-435 looked like a parking lot. People were riding each other's bumpers while battering their horns at one another as tensions rose. One motorist rear-ended another right in the middle of the highway.

"Lawd, why in front of me? I got places to be!"

Two big, angry men stepped out of a brand-new pearl-colored Cadillac Escalade. The motorist who hit the SUV could be seen locking his doors and moving over to the passenger side of his vehicle. The big man on the left began to knock rapidly on the window while his friend rattled the door of the mid-sized sedan.

The scared motorist cracked his window and informed the guys that he was calling 911 while shaking his cell phone in their direction. The driver of the SUV inspected his ride to assess the damages and then went back to confront the motorist again. The scared motorist panicked and jumped out of the passenger side door, then took off running down the off ramp.

I was sitting directly behind all of the drama that took place. All I needed was a bag of popcorn, some peanut M&M's, a super-sized cola and I would be set without even needing a big screen. I couldn't believe ol' boy just left his car in the middle of the highway and took off.

'How am I supposed to get around all this mess?' I thought rolling my eyes.

The driver of the Escalade looked back and glared my way. He then signaled to his friend to give him a minute and walked toward my vehicle. He stood at least 6'1"and weighed about 300 pounds solid.

I tried to swallow the lump that was stuck in my throat while keeping my eyes from popping out their sockets. He stopped at my car door and then motioned for me to roll my window down. I guess I was taking too long, so he knocked again and said, "Crack your window."

Momma didn't raise a fool so I lowered my window just an inch.

"Yes?" I said in a somewhat annoyed voice.

"How are you today, Ms. Lady" he said, while looking back at his dog to show him that he was about to get his mack on.

"It depends."

'My mouth has always gotten me into trouble,' I thought to myself.

He then laughed at that comment and said, "I'm harmless, really."

My face probably looked like I was in the midst of a "yeah right" moment. He laughed once again.

"Look, beautiful," he said, "I just want to help you back up your ride so you won't be stuck behind jackass who bailed out. No harm intended."

Feeling somewhat safe, I exhaled.

"I'm sorry that I lost my cool," he said. "I had just purchased my ride yesterday and drove it off the showroom floor an hour ago. Dude scratched my rear bumper and was going to drive off. Can you believe that?" he asked.

"In this day and time, I wouldn't put anything past anyone!" I stated while I also assessed his damages.

"It's going to cost me a cool mint to get it fixed," he whined.

"From the looks of it, it doesn't look like you're hurting for cash," I smiled.

"Yeah, you know a brotha's gotta do what a brotha's gotta do," he announced with a sly grin on his face.

All while I was chatting with "Mr. Tall, Dark and Handsome," traffic was at a standstill. Irritated motorists began to blare their horns in frustration. Many, I was sure were late for work —along with me.

I could tell that he was loaded like an ATM from the flashy display of a huge platinum and diamond crusted necklace he was wearing. The diamond medallion was shaped in the form of the letters B&R. He wore a pair of dark-colored slacks, a white cotton shirt and a black thigh-length mink. He smelled good, too. I got a brief whiff of his cologne and recognized the scent to be Cool Water. He wore a low-cut fade that looked freshly trimmed. His smooth dark-brown skin was radiant in the mid-morning sun.

I must say, baby boy was fine.

I snapped back to reality when he asked for my name.
"Brooke and yours I asked?"

"They call me Deuce-Deuce, but you can call me Dante'.
It's a pleasure meeting you, Brooke. Where's a luscious lady
like you off to this hectic Monday morning?"

"I was on my way to work and I'm really late. Right now
I'll get there when I get there given the circumstances."

He licked his thick, brown lips and asked, "Can I take
you out to a nice dinner and movie, sometime?"

I give him an *'umm hum'* look that caused another round
of laughter from him.

"No, seriously, I'm harmless and just want to have the
chance to entertain a lovely woman such as you. Here's my
business card with my office, cell phone and home phone
numbers. You can reach me at any one no matter the time of
day," he said.

I took his card and glanced out of the corner of my eye.

"Well, Dante', I'll give you a call later on," I said, which
made him smile flashing a set of pearly white teeth.

"Well, let me help you back up so folks can stop honking
and you can finally get to work."

He helped me back out and waved good-bye as I tooted
my horn and rushed down the highway towards work. I
glanced down at his card and saw his title, underneath his
name, read "President of Blazin' Records."

I couldn't be mad at a brother for doing his thing. *'What
harm could it be to go out and enjoy a night on the town
with a nice-looking man?'* I shook my head and smiled all
the way to my job.

Chapter Six
Can I Take You Out Tonight?

I glanced at myself from my bedroom mirror. I turned around to catch a glimpse of my butt to see if it stuck out too far in the form-fitting, DKNY little black dress.

'I thought black was supposed to make you look thinner? I'll remember to thank my parents for this thick kadonkadonk.'

Oh well. I was always told to make the best of what I had.

"Okay, I think I'm doing this black dress justice," I said into the mirror.

I looked at my shoe rack and tried to pick a pair that would accessorize the mess out of my outfit.

"Sexy but comfy, girl!" I joked in regards to my dogs. "I don't want them barking before leaving out the front door."

I found the perfect pair that I had purchased last summer that I never wore.

"Too cute; can't believe I haven't worn these."

The shoes were open-toed black-strapped heels that fastened around my ankle. The shoes showed off my shapely calves and put some height to my 5'4" 185 pound frame.

Earlier in the day, I went to the salon to get my hair shampooed and styled in loose curly ringlets. As I applied the last coat of MAC lip-gloss to my lips, I heard my doorbell ring. I could see that Dante' was very punctual, which was an A-plus in my book. I swung my chocolate kadonkadonk side-to-side en route to the front door.

Surprised, I was greeted by a bouquet of purple and red roses.

"Well, good evening, luscious," Dante' said licking his lips like he was LL Cool J as he handed me the beautiful bouquet.

"Come in and make yourself comfortable. Can I get you a drink? I have bottled water, soda, and something stronger, if you like."

"A glass of water is fine for me," he said while pressing out his jeans with his hands trying to stay so fresh and so clean, I guessed. I turned and went into the kitchen and could feel him staring at me all the way there. I returned and handed him his water.

"Thank you," he said grinning at me.

"So, what's the plan for us tonight," I asked.

"It's a surprise. You'll see. I want to make it a night that you can remember."

"Okay, well let me grab my wrap and purse then we can head out."

He helped put my wrap around my shoulders and, as I turned to face him, he planted a soft kiss near the corner of my lips.

'*He's too smooth,*" I thought.

After I resumed breathing, I managed to ask him, "Ready to head out?"

"After you," he said and let me lead the way to his ride parked in my driveway.

I noticed that Dante' had a different whip. This time, he was sporting silver-painted Dodge Charger with black leather seats.

I slid into the passenger seat, while holding all of me in trying to preserve the sexy as much as possible while he held the door open. I admired the interior of his car that was equipped with some extra goodies that were installed.

It seemed as if Dante' was doing well for himself.

He walked around to the driver's side and slipped off his jacket in order to get comfortable while driving, then started the Charger. The velvety voice of Rachelle Farrell flowed from his surround-sound stereo speakers. I snapped my fingers to the beat of the music and hummed along to a familiar song.

Dante' curled his lips into a sly smile and glanced my way.

"I see you like my girl Rachelle. She's one of the best jazz singers out there today."

"I have to agree with you on that one. She has collaborated with many well-known artists. I love a couple that she's done with Will Downing. She has a rich voice that can calm a storm and I would love to see her perform live," I said.

"Beautiful woman, great legs and good taste in music, I think I met my match," he playfully said.

He then reached over and intertwined his fingers with mine as we rode in silence and listened to music.

We arrived at an upscale restaurant located on the west side of town. As Dante' got out, a valet opened my door and greeted me. Dante' was waiting and took my hand to lead me into the restaurant.

In total awe, I took in my new surroundings. The restaurant was dimly lit with vanilla-scented candles. We were led to a private area encased with flowing sheer curtains on each side. Dante' took my wrap and waited until I was seated before he handed it over to our server.

"Hello Mr. Hunter," our server said. "It's nice to see you again. Would you like to view the wine menu?"

"The usual will do, Patrick. Would you also please check to see if Pedro is working tonight? I would thank him for the tip he gave me several weeks ago. It panned out well for me and I have a little token of my appreciation to give him."

"Yes sir. Right away," the server replied. "I'll return with the wine in just a few. Here are your menus."

'This place is amazing," I said looking around. "I see that you come here often."

"Actually, I hold my monthly meetings here and entertain VIPs who come into town every so often. I'm usually in another part of the restaurant that holds more than twenty people. I only had the chance to eat in this private area twice —this being the second time."

I raised one eyebrow and asked boldly, "Who was your first?"

He belted out a strong, hearty laugh and shook his head as if I told him a joke.

"It was a special person from my past —my ex-fiancé."

'Okay Brooke, don't raise the eye, girl! Play along.'

"Fiancé, you were engaged?" I blurted.

"Yes, a few years ago, but things didn't work out," he said with a distant look on his face.

"Who broke off the engagement; you or her?"

"I did after I caught her cheating with her ex-boyfriend at my crib. I was out of town on business and came back home a few days earlier than expected. I wanted to surprise her and take her to the Bahamas with me and walked in on her and old dude knocking the bedbugs off the sheets!"

'See it's stupid stuff like that that will twist a man and his trust factor with ALL women up. Okay, now I see I gotta pass his tests. Hope he is aware that I have not only a high school education, but college, as well! I'm done with school!'

"Dang, for real? Are you serious?" I asked.

"Yes, it really happened. Before I knew it, I had grabbed him by the neck and threw him out of my condo only with the skin that he was born in," Dante' said. "My ex kept begging me not to hurt him. Dude was screaming like a girl when I threw his lanky behind against the wall. In that little time it took to throw her boy out, she managed to put on some sweats, a tee shirt and tennis shoes. I told her she might as well bounce, that I would pack her things and that I'd send them to her. She grabbed his clothes and stormed out of the house. She slammed the door so hard, my good artwork, framed in pure gold, fell to the floor!

"It took a long time for me to get over her betrayal. I gave my all to that girl and expected no less from her," he said. "Like they say, 'Time heals all wounds.' Now it's time for me to move on to bigger and better things."

He reached for my hand and kissed my palm.

'Is it hot in here or what?' I thought.

I begin to fan myself with my free hand. As he was about to say something, the waiter came over to our table and placed our wine and bread down. He also alerted Dante' that Pedro would be out shortly and he wanted to give us a few more moments to look at our menus.

"What do you suggest I request, Dante'?" I asked peering over the menu.

"The Chicken Marsala with Fettuccini Alfredo is excellent and so is the stuffed manicotti," he responded.

I debated on which to choose from and ended up selecting the Marsala as he suggested. Dante' chose the same and then handed both our menus to our server.

"Now, where was I?" he asked taking my hands into his.

"Bigger and better!" I cheerfully remind him. "Right," he said looking me directly in the eye.

"You have beautiful brown eyes; people would pay money to have eyes like yours."

"I bet you jive all the ladies who flaunt a big butt and a smile," I joked. We both laughed, then I realized how serious he was.

"You're a special woman who I'd like to get to know beyond just a friendship," he said. "I'm a patient man who is down to earth. No pressure, I would just like to get to know you better if you're okay with it."

"I have to admit something to you, Dante'; at first, I thought that you were a dope-selling-money-making thug. "Looks can be deceiving," he said. "Plus, society has jacked us all up with stereotyping people."

"True," I said. "Let me be the first to say that I'm sorry for assuming the worst of your character."

"No offense taken, baby girl. I know that I may come off rough and mean but, in my business, I have to so the knuckleheads won't try to step to me wrong. Believe me when I say that I'm a pussycat when it comes to my woman. "I can't put my finger on it, Brooke; I just like your style and want to get to know you better."

"Well, so far, I'm enjoying your company and I'm willing to get to know you better; one step at a time."

"Well, let's toast to the beginning of a new friendship."

We lifted both our wine glasses and clicked them against one another.

"Cheers."

For the rest of the evening, we enjoyed each other's company while getting to know one another better. I hadn't felt so free since my divorce —free to be the Brooke who was hidden during my marriage to Jonathan.

'Could Dante' be 'the one?'" I pondered.

Only time would tell which path we would travel.

The temperature had dropped about fifteen degrees by the time Dante' and I left the restaurant. I huddled near Dante' because my wrap was not warm enough while we waited for the valet to bring the Charger around front. As the Valet held the door open for me, I felt the warmth from the heater in the car. Dante' tipped the valet driver a twenty dollar bill.

"Thank you, sir, and I hope you and your lady have a great evening," the valet said.

"Thanks, my man, and take care," Dante' responded as he slid into the driver's side of the car.

"I had a fabulous time at dinner," I said settling in for a toasty ride. "The meal was great and the ambience was out of this world."

We cruised towards the streets of downtown. I was in a relaxed mood and enjoying the time that I was spending with Dante' until his cell phone rang. As he looked at the caller ID on his cell phone, I saw that the muscles in his jaws tightened. He then let out a long sigh and finally pushed the

"Talk" button as he held the phone to his ear. In a voice that was filled with frustration, he said, "Hello" to the person on the other end of the line. After several seconds of silence, he told the caller that he was busy and that he couldn't talk right then. The caller seemed to be persistent because Dante' asked, "Did you hear what I just said!" then asked the caller what the reason for calling was.

"Look, you had your chance and blew it and I don't have time for your type of drama and madness."

After several seconds he said, "Look I have company and I told you that now is not the time. I'll check back with you in a couple of days."

He pushed the "End" button.

Dante' shook his head in disbelief and then slapped the steering wheel as he pulled the car over to the side of the road.

"Is everything okay with you?" I nervously asked. "No, but it will be. I shouldn't let people get me so frustrated. I'm having the time of my life with you, Brooke, and I do not want the rest of our evening to be ruined.

"You're a cool person to me and I really do like you as well as enjoy your company," he said while massaging his temples.

"That was my ex-fiancé on the phone. She has been leaving messages at my office and leaving me emails stating that we need to talk and it can't wait. She knew she messed up royally and I won't stand for nonsense! Like I told you at dinner, I've moved on to bigger and better things," he said and kissed my hand.

"Thank you for being honest. I can appreciate that," I told him. "I've been in a similar situation. The ex will not leave you alone because they suddenly realize that they have messed up a good thing. As a matter of fact, it's my ex-husband who doesn't have a clue."

"You've been married before?" he asked.

"Yes I have—for ten years. I was in a marriage that went nowhere. I gave him the boot and never turned back. Now that I think about it, I stayed in that marriage for all the wrong reasons. I'm at a happy place in my life and don't want to lose that feeling by taking three steps backwards and give him another chance to repeat the same things he did wrong all over again."

"I feel you on that one. You are way too beautiful to be neglected and abused. Hopefully, you'll give me a chance to show you that there are still good men out there who know how to treat a woman," Dante' said.

He had me blushing and feeling giggly inside. I could respect a man who was honest and truthful.

"I'd rather be hurt by the truth than hurt by a lie," I told him.

"I'm not here to hurt you darling, I just want to get to know you better and be more than just a friend to you if allow me to do so," he said.

He leaned over and kissed me softly on the lips. As I leaned in closer, I took in his scent, which smelled fresh like the ocean on a summer afternoon. We kissed for what seemed liked forever. It was sizzling in the car — and not from the heat that was blowing from the vents. He then kissed my neck and mumbled that I smelled good. My breathing became more labored when he slowly departed from my neck and returned to my lips again.

After several minutes, we embraced and looked one another in the eye.

"I better get you home before I get you into trouble," he said.

"Yes, that's a great idea," I replied while caressing his well-trimmed beard.

He hesitated for a moment then smiled and pulled away from the curb continuing toward my house. I leaned back and relaxed my head on the headrest of the car and then closed my eyes to listen to Kenny G perform live in concert. My eyes were getting heavy and the warmth from the car put me to sleep. I woke to soft, subtle lips kissing my check and Dante' calling my name.

"We're here," he said.

I looked out of the window and sadly asked, "So soon? I'm sorry that I fell asleep."

"No problem baby girl," he said smiling. "You looked so peaceful as you slept— I didn't want to wake you."

"I want to thank you, again, for such a great evening," I told him. "I needed to get out and enjoy myself instead of working all the time."

"We both needed time away from our busy schedules," he said as he helped me with my wrap then opened the passenger door. "Hopefully, this won't be the last time."

I grabbed my keys from inside of my purse to unlock my door. Dante' was so close behind me that I could feel the warmth of his body. After unlocking my front door, I turned around to face him and give him a hug.

"I'll call you tomorrow afternoon if that's okay with you," he said. "Maybe we can get together later on in the week and have lunch, dinner or breakfast, Ms. Lady."

"You're a naughty boy Dante' and, yes, I will accept your invitation as long as you behave."

"Scout's honor!" he said and quickly raised two fingers together as if he was giving a pledge.

"Take care, Ms. Lady, and I'll see you soon."

"Goodnight Dante'!" I happily stated as I watched him approach his car. He looked back my way and waved before he got into his car. I closed my front door and fell back on it with my hand across my chest. I was filled with excitement and anticipation. I couldn't wait to call Gabby and tell her about the great time I spent with Dante'. I headed toward my bedroom while singing, "What a man what man what a man, what a mighty good man."

Chapter Seven
What People Say

I was rubbing my temples so hard that I thought I just placed a dent on both sides of my head. Talking very loudly — as always—on the phone was Mr. Billings, the account manager for the law firm I worked for. As a fellow employee, Mr. Billings was over the new client in-take and oversaw financial matters when hiring interns.

His news was not good. He told me that he couldn't afford to hire a new assistant for the summer internship program, which our firm hosted each summer. I had interviewed several prospective students and narrowed my search down to two fresh— but smart and hardworking — college graduates.

I questioned him as to why the funds were available for last year and not again for the upcoming summer program.

He went on to tell me that the firm was planning to cut back— if not eliminate— many of the funded programs for the low-income clients. I asked him why they couldn't cut back on employee raises and company-paid trips to many of the unnecessary conferences hosted each year in Hawaii.

"I don't see where a company-paid trip is relevant and any of your business, Brooke!" he said.

"It's Ms. Henderson to you!" I snapped and proceeded to slam the phone onto the hook.

'His arrogant, receding hair line, bifocal wearing, old dingy Danny Glover looking-ass fool!'

I picked up the phone and slammed it down quite a few times more to get my point across.

Who was I kidding— he pissed me off!

I opened my desk drawer and rambled through it until I found my happy pills. I hadn't taken one of those since being married to Jonathan. Mr. Billings had me so stressed out that I was starting to see double.

I cared about all people— even the snooty-rich pricks that came in the office looking for help to get off on drama that could qualify them for a first-class, roundtrip, nonstop ticket to hell!

'What do I tell people now? We are known for helping low-income and underprivileged people.'

I was so angry that I felt heat rising from the tips of my ears. I leaned back in my seat and closed my eyes until my happy pills took effect.

"There must be a way to help new and old clients out," I said to myself. "I'll find a way even if I have to hustle and generate funds myself."

'Dear old Mr. Billings hasn't heard the last from me,' I thought determinedly.

I picked up the phone and began to dial the number to my supervisor's office. A knock on my office door interrupted my dialing.

"Come in, it's open," I said and placed the phone back on its base. Shelia, my secretary, entered with a wide grin on her face while holding a huge floral arrangement filled with vibrant spring flowers.

"Someone must have been really nice!" she teased and set the vase on my desk. "A florist delivered these to you while you were on the phone."

"Thanks, Shelia," I said while removing the card that came with the floral arrangement.

"Enjoy, I'm going to lunch," she said. "Page me if you need something."

I read the note and realized that it was from Dante'.

It read: *"Thank you, special lady, for gracing me with your presence last night. I truly enjoyed your company and great conversation. I hope that your night was also a pleasant one and I can't wait to see you again. I will be flying out of town tomorrow to meet with a prospective client and will be back this weekend. I'll give you a call once I get settled in my room, lovely lady. I hope you like the flowers. They remind me of you. Until we meet again,*
Dante'"

The man was good. I read the card and sniffed the inside of it. I smelled the scent of Cool Water once again. I grabbed my billfold and took the business card out that Dante' had given me on the day we met, then dialed his office number that was listed on it. After several rings, the receptionist answered the phone.

"Blazin' Records. How may I direct your call?" she asked.

"Yes, may I speak with Dante' Hunter," I said.

"May I ask who's calling"?

"Brooke Henderson," I said.

"Please hold."

After several seconds, Dante's baritone voice was on the other end of my line saying, "Hello baby girl. How are you today?"

"I'm great especially after receiving this magnificent floral arrangement."

"You like them," he asked.

"Yes, I do and the card was wonderful."

"I'm glad that you got them before I left town. I had to tip the deliveryman a twenty spot to have them to you today instead of tomorrow since they were closing for the day."

"Thank you so much Dante'. I am pleasantly surprised and the flowers smell so good."

We chatted for several minutes before he realized that he needed to go home and change to prepare for his flight.

"I'll call you sometime around mid-afternoon tomorrow," he said.

"That's fine by me," I said. "Have a safe trip."

"Thanks, baby girl. I will talk to you soon."

We both said our goodbyes. I placed the phone back on its base and stared at my flowers again.

I had to wonder where all of this was going and whether or not I was ready to jump back into a relationship again. I was a little nervous and the butterflies that went along with that appeared in my belly. I felt that it was best to take my time and not rush into things too quickly. Dante' was a wonderful man and knew how to, definitely, treat a woman, but that ex of his popped into my mind.

'Was she going to be a problem? I am very leery of being hurt again!'

I did not know how recent their break-up was and if he was truly over being hurt by the woman who he had intended to spend his life with.

"Your life with?" was deep right there all by itself.

I planned on mentally moving out of the fast lane to the right side of the road to the slower lanes.

"Take your time; take your time, Brooke," I whispered to myself as I read his card again.

Chapter Eight
The Man Behind His Words

The day was long and stressful for me. I was trying to wrap things up at the office as quickly as I could, but felt like I'd never escape the place. I logged on to my computer to check for any last-minute emails. After reading several from various department heads, I saw that Myles left me an email.

I had been so busy the past several days and hadn't logged on to check my messages for some time. His email said that he enjoyed chatting with me and, if I was on Yahoo!, to be sure to hit him up. He also stated that he was able to read the poetry that I sent him and longed to read more. I had sent him several of my poems and wanted his opinion about them. I felt it was good considering he loved music and he wrote from time-to-time, himself. Some of his poems were erotic and sensual while others were poetic and mysterious.

I logged on to check my Yahoo! Messenger to see if he was online.

thickwitit32: "Hello Myles, how are you this evening?" I typed.

Compozer: "I'm doing well. It's great to hear from you. How has your day been so far?"

I told him about the events that took place with Mr. Billings and how I was on the phone for most of the day trying to find ways to build funds for our low-income clients. He was sorry to hear of the company cutting the funds and wished me well with the fundraising. He then typed that he had a few of the artists that he worked with who might be interested in donating funds. I told him that any help would be greatly appreciated and whatever he came up with was better than no help at all.

I asked how his day was progressing and he told me that he met with a record label to discuss a recording contract.

Compozer: *"Things went well for me today and, hopefully, the record executives would get back with me, soon. In the meantime, I still have to put bread on the table and bills to pay and that's why my main job is with this advertising agency. I like my job and it's a good way to express some of my creativity, but my true calling is my music. I express myself so much better through music."*

As I read Myles' comments about his music, I envisioned him behind a baby grand piano toggling the ebony and ivory keys. I wanted to hear him play live or, at least, hear a sample of his music. So I typed in a sentence and, before I knew it, clicked the "Send" button.

thickwitit32: *"You have piqued an interest for me about your music. I wonder if I could listen to some of your work and hear the voice of the man behind the words."*

Compozer: *"Yes, anytime you like."*

thickwitit32: *"I will email you my number and I'll include the best time to reach me."*

That move surprised even me. I wasn't usually that straight forward and was certainly not the one who would be the aggressor.

We wrapped up our chat session. I told him that it-was time for me to head home and that I looked forward to his phone call. We said our goodbyes and I logged off my computer. I grabbed my purse and a few files that I had to work on while at home. I headed down to the main lobby and said my usual end-of-day pleasantries to the night security guard.

"Have a safe ride home, Ms. Henderson," he said while holding the door open for me.

I clicked the alarm on my SUV and placed my files and purse on the passenger side. It was rather cool outside so I sat for a few minutes to let my truck warm up. As I pulled away from my parking spot, I grinned as I tripped off the bold way that I passed my number along to Myles. My mom would have called me a playette.

'Yes, that's a new word—add it to your vocab."

I would say, "It's just a way to meet new friends."

I found the Internet to be a harmless way to be able to converse with people who lived in different parts of the world. I realized that there were crazy folks running up and down the highways of the internet pretending to be sane, sexy and super which, all three, end up turning up to be crazy, butt-ugly and weak as hell! Still, it was something about Myles that made me want to know, not just about the musician, but also about the man behind his words.

I turned on my CD player and sang along with my girl, Mary J, on my way to home sweet home.

"It's the weekend baby!" I sang to myself while twisting my hips with my hands in the air as if I was at some hot concert. The past week had been really stressful for me with all the budget cuts and dealing with Mr. Billings. I had to go over his head to get the needed approval for the two clients we saw prior to him cutting funds. I called the two clients and informed them of their attorneys working their cases.

One client was an African-American male— about seventeen years of age —who was choked by his history teacher. Apparently, the teacher and the student never got along, but saying, "Nigger shut up and sit your 'Boyz in the Hood' ass down!" does not justify a damn thing. I would not have cared if the boy came at him with a baseball bat— there's just some things that don't need to be said. I couldn't blame the kid for trying to beat up that man. I was glad we had proof of the man making a statement like that.

The other client—all I could say was that I wished Johnny Cochran was alive. A thirty-three-year-old woman accused of abusing her foster kids was her scenario. There were conflicting stories, but it seemed all family and neighbors agreed that she loved those kids and would never let harm come on the same street she lived on.

'Lord help us!'

I finally made it home after battling rush-hour traffic on the road and in the grocery store. I grabbed enough groceries for a week to keep from having to make repeat trips.

After checking the mail and phone messages, once home, I showered and changed into a comfortable pair of shorts and a tank top. I headed into the kitchen and started to prepare dinner. I decided to make a beef and broccoli stir fry served with brown rice pilaf. As I was grabbing the veggies from the refrigerator, the telephone rang. I looked at the caller ID when it came up unavailable. I was thinking that it might have been a telemarketer and so I answered with the "you're bothering me" attitude.

"Hi, may I speak with Brooke?" the mellow voice asked.

"May I ask who's calling?"

"This is Myles," he said in a sexy, deep, and mellow voice.

I almost dropped the cordless phone and had to juggle the vegetables so I wouldn't drop them, too. His voice had a deep, rich tone that sent chill down my arms. In a brief second, I managed to gather myself and paced my breathing so my voice wouldn't sound shaky.

"This is Brooke," I replied coolly. "How are you this evening Myles?"

"I'm doing magnificent now that I'm able to hear your voice, Beautiful!"

I started thinking to myself, *'Brothaman has skills, flirting and is throwing his mack down.'*

"Well that's good to hear," he said.

"How have things been for you? I know that it's been a couple of days since we last chatted online, but we both have hectic and busy schedules," I said.

"Yes, this week has truly been a busy one for me," Myles said. I've met with the record executives again this week and they gave the okay for my CD. I start recording next week and will be out of town for several weeks. I also have to let my band know of the upcoming recording event so that they can clear their schedules and be available for during the weeks ahead."

"Congratulations! I'm happy for you and I know that you're excited. I would love the chance to hear some of your music since jazz is one of my favorite genres of music."

"Tell you what; I'll send you a few of my songs by email later on tonight."

"Great," I said and told him to send the files to my Yahoo! email address.

"So why aren't you out painting the town tonight?" He asked.

"I'm a home-body and I don't do much clubbing unless I'm out celebrating with one of my home girls."

"I hear you on that one. I'd rather be at home than performing from one club to another. I'm trying to get my music out there and, so far, I have gotten good response from many jazz lovers. But, when it's all said and done, I still don't have anyone special to share my good news with," he said.

"I'm surprised that you don't. An attractive man, such as yourself, should have been snatched up a long time ago. I'm sure you have plenty of women who would love to get the chance to share your good news with," I said.

We both laughed.

"You would be surprised at the women who throw themselves at musicians. I take it all with a grain of salt. When I'm done performing, I pack up and leave as soon as possible. In the past, I had a bad experience with a stalker who I let buy me a drink. We dated for a short time until I broke it off when she became too controlling and wanted to know my every move. To this day, she still stalks me and follows my band from one gig to another," he said.

I made a mental note to self: *"Dear Self, possible nut case on the loose!"*

"Since that, I've been very selective about who I consider dating and I'm upfront about my expectations. I've never been the type of man who would hit it and quit it or act like a player, player! I'm not that type of man. Sometimes musicians get a bad name and women usually think that we have a woman in every state that we have a gig in. So for now, I'm single and concentrating exclusively on my music."

"I can feel you on that one. I know how it is to be in a relationship only to find out that you totally wasted time and energy. I'm very picky when it comes to a certain kind of man that I will date. I know that everyone has their flaws here and there, and that there's no such thing as the perfect man, however, I would like to meet a man who has qualities that I have— you know a man like yourself."

'Did I say that last statement out loud?'

Myles started chuckling.

"So am I," he stated.

"Well, all righty then!" I said in order to move on and not let the conversation too serious.

I asked him if he'd been married before and he responded, "Yes.

"I was married for five years and have two beautiful girls. They are my pride and joy and the reason that I am grounded and stable. My oldest daughter is seven and the youngest is four."

"Do they reside with you I asked?"

"No, they live with my ex and her mother. She also has an older son from a previous relationship whom I considered to be my own. Although we live in two different states, I try to call as much as possible and fly out to see them every few months when time permits. It's hard not being able to see them like I used to when I was married to their mother."

"So what happened to make you all call it a quits?"

"We just fell apart throughout the years. It felt like we were roommates instead of husband and wife. She felt that other things in her life were more important than being a wife and, when I asked her did she still love me, she stated that she loved her mission more than she loved me.

"It hurt hearing that, but I already knew the answer before I asked her. I wanted to hear her say it instead of me trying to salvage our marriage only not to prevail. A few months later, I had the opportunity to join a band that was well-known in Detroit and I jumped on it. It was difficult in the beginning. I was trying to adjust not being able to see my girls every day. It was extremely hard on me. I called them several times a day just to hear their little voices say, 'Hi daddy.' That was all I wanted to hear.

"I plan to travel their way this summer for a few days and surprise them for their birthdays, which are a week apart."

"I know that they will be happy to see their daddy," I said. "Seems like they have you wrapped around their little sweet fingers."

"You got that right!" he said. "I've already made a huge dent with my credit card buying gifts and clothes but, you know, I couldn't have it any other way."

"I can admire a man who holds down his responsibilities because of love and not because a judge ordered him to do so," I said. "Some men gripe about having to pay child support for their children even when they had a hand— well, more than that — in bringing them into this world.

"You deserve great applause for being an awesome dad. Your girls will remember this when they grow older and choose a man to marry. Having a dad who is active in a girl's life determines what kind of man she chooses, in my opinion. I know that if my dad were around, I would have made a better choice in the men I dated and with the one I married."

"That's so very true," he said. "But, I don't expect a pat on the back for what I do. It's my responsibility to make sure that they are provided for and taken into consideration in many of the choices that I make. My girls are the center of my life and shall always be. Unfortunately, I still have to deal with their mother. She makes things more difficult than they should be. Although I may not reside in the same state, I practically still pay her living expenses as if I still live there.

"I informed her to get prepared to take care of her own self. As far as things go, my obligations are to my children only— not to her and her gold-digging mother.

"I guess a lot of this may be my fault."

"How so?" I asked.

"When we started having children, I wanted her to stay home to avoid sending the girls off to a lazy sicko to look after my children. People are nowhere what they used to be! She agreed and stated that being at home with the girls, also, would save us money. I didn't trust many babysitters or daycare providers to look after and care for my children— especially after hearing on the news about children being neglected and abused by daycare providers," he said. "What my ex-wife fails to understand is that I have to survive and make ends meet for myself. I'm a man with needs, wants and desires. She is capable of working now, especially since the girls are of school age.

"What she does with her time all day never fails to amaze me. She didn't clean and I had to cook for myself when we were married. I know that she spent a lot of her time chanting and talking on the phone to her so-called gospel physic phone-line."

"Gospel Physic hotline?" I asked with a chuckle. "What was that all about?"

"Well, she started a hotline for callers to get spiritual advice and she would — to a certain extent— predict the outcome of it all. That's when I realized that she was a couple of sandwiches short of a picnic," he said.

I almost choked on my cranberry juice that I was sipping on when he said that.

'Thank God for the mute button!'

"She took her work seriously and felt that I should back her up financially and fund her eccentric goal to reach out and give spiritual advice to 'lost souls'— her words exactly.

My job as a husband and father was to provide for my family; not host her fly-by-night adventures."

"Does she still have her hotline? I asked.

"No, but she claims to still practice her saving souls mission. I don't really get involved in her mission and I know who my Lord is and what He is capable of. My religious belief is totally different than what she conceives it to be.

"My ex-wife never attended worship services with the girls and me; she felt that she could benefit better staying at home rather than worship with other parishioners. So, eventually, she did her own thing and I did mine. I hate to have havoc and drama in my life and I try to avoid it at any cost. I guess that's why I'm still single at this point in my life. The next woman I choose to be my wife will be grounded and know what she wants out of life.

"I want her to have the same goals and dreams that I have. I've been hurt too many times and now I'm selective about women who I date. I know that's a lot to take in but I won't settle for any less than a woman would expect from me," He stated.

"I can understand what you mean, Myles," I said. "Many people out there are rushing into relationships just for the sake of having someone. You have to be selective of the type of person that you date or choose to have a relationship with.

"I have always seen myself as a wife to a good man. I married someone who I thought would appreciate that. My ex-husband failed to mature on the same level I was. Hell, he was older than me! We were childhood sweethearts since the ages of ten and eleven. I was mistaken to think that, when he got older, he would be responsible and would put me first as his wife. I soon found out other things were more important to him than being a husband and a provider. It took me awhile to realize that I could do much better and didn't have to put up with his abuse, excessive drinking, and his extra-marital affairs. I know that divorcing him and moving on was the best thing for me and I'm extremely happy for it.

"Being single is by choice, at this point in my life, and I date casually but nothing serious. Like you, I'm very picky about who I will date and refuse to settle for less than my standards," I said.

"Well it seems like we would make the perfect match, Brooke," he said with a hearty laugh.

'Man, this brother keeps sending chills down my arms. I have to get off this phone before I say something I might regret.'

"We just may make the perfect match for one another," I said, then joked: "Hey, let's call your ex-wife for some physic advice."

We couldn't help but to laugh loudly and I couldn't control the next round of laughter after he started laughing again. I had stomach cramps and told him to stop acting up before I pass out from lack of oxygen.

After we gained control of ourselves, I told Myles that I had to go before I burned my dinner for the night. He apologized for keeping me on the phone for so long. I told him that the pleasure was all mine and that I truly enjoyed talking and laughing with him.

"May I call you again tomorrow evening?" he asked.

"Sure, anytime that you please. I had a ball chatting with you. Take care, Myles, and have a pleasant evening."

"I know that I've talked with a lovely lady who made me smile. Goodnight, Brooke. I shall talk with you soon."

After I said, "Goodnight" we both ended our connection to one another. The corners of my lips were hurting because I couldn't seem to wipe the smile from my face. I looked forward to speaking with him again I thought as I set my dinner table for one.

Chapter Nine
The Knock Out

I managed to bump my head against the headboard after being startled by a knock on my bedroom window. I had a feeling that I'd have a nasty bump on my head by mid-morning. I sat up and stared straight ahead like a deer in headlights.

'Who, in the hell, was knocking on my window at two in the morning?'

I heard a knock once again followed by my ex-husband saying, "Baby, baby, let me in."

I snatched the covers back and quickly ran to the window to pull the blinds aside.

"What the hell you want? Why are you knocking on my damn window at two a.m.?"

I could tell that he was under the influence by the way that he swayed like a leaf in a windstorm. He held a brown paper bag in one hand, which also let me know that he was toting some cheap drink.

"Jonathan, you know that you're not allowed any contact with me whatsoever. I'm sick of you ignoring the restraining order by thinking that you are above the law. You need to leave before I call the police and have you arrested," I angrily stated.

The scene made me flashback to those hell-awful days of that so-called sacred matrimony.

"I just want to make things right with you and get my baby back," he whined.

Next, the dumb fool started to bellow—okay sing —the theme song from some restaurant commercial.

"I want my baby back, baby back, baby back."

He then burst out in a round of drunken laughter at his own heckling. When he finally took control of himself, he staggered over to the nearest tree and relieved his bladder. After adjusting himself, he took another swig from his beer bottle. I couldn't stand the man. His drunken adventures were one of the reasons that I divorced his sorry behind.

He then staggered to my window and said, "Now where was I? Oh yeah, I want to make what I did wrong to you right and show you that I've changed."

"You have got to be kidding me," I said. "You are positively, absolutely out of your drunk mind. As far as I know, hell hasn't frozen over yet and that would be the only way that I would allow you to bring drama back into my life. You made my life a living hell and there is no way that you and I will ever get back together! What you need to do is get away from my window, better yet, away from my house and crawl back under the rock that you came from!"

"All right, all right, I'm leaving," he said. "You don't have to call the police. I'll stop bothering you."

He walked away towards his car that was parked on the other side of the street in the wrong direction.

"What a loser," I mumbled under my breath as he walked away.

While walking back to my bed, I managed to stub my toe and trip over the throw rug all while trying to keep my balance.

"Urghh, that man frustrates me to no limit!" I screamed out loud.

Next time that Jonathan came by —or even said one word to me—I vowed that I would call the police.

No sooner than I got back comfortable, I heard a loud crash from outside. I took hold of my robe and headed towards the living room and looked out the window only to see Jonathan throwing a large rock at my Navigator windows. I saw that he managed to knock out the rear side passenger window and was aiming at the front windshield. I took my cordless phone, ran back to my room and grabbed the bat that I kept under my bed, slipped on my tennis shoes, and headed for the front door. I heard another huge explosion and saw glass flying in a million pieces as I stepped out the front door.

The fool managed to break every last window in my SUV except the rear window.

There the nut stood in my driveway breathless from the chaos he started.

"I told you that you were my property and that you will always belong to me," he snarled then took another swig of his beer and stood back to survey and applaud himself for the damage that he'd done to my truck.

I was glad that I had slept in my shorts and tee shirt because I planned on doing a Babe Ruth on his ass. He was too busy laughing and drinking his beer to notice that I was coming in his direction. My first swing landed on his right arm. He dropped his brown paper bag and grabbed his right arm. I then took another swing and landed a huge blow to his kneecap.

~CRACK~

That was the sound I heard as he fell to the ground and began to wail like a two-year-old child. I stood over him and looked him straight in the eye.

"Negro, if you ever, ever come by my house again and destroy any of my property, you will be carried away by the medical examiner instead of an ambulance. Is that understood?" I asked while I nudged him with the tip of the baseball bat.

He cried out, "Yes, while holding his injured knee."

"Good, so we don't have any misunderstandings do we?" I asked before I walked away.

As I reached my front door, I heard sirens about a block away. I guess one of my many nosey neighbors called the police before I had the chance to. I grabbed my purse to retrieve my copy of the restraining order to show the police when they arrive. I put my bat under my bed and waited by the front door. Several police cars arrived on the scene and a few surveyed the damage while others were walking towards Jonathan who was still screaming like a woman at the top of his lungs. One officer could be heard calling to dispatch asking them to send an ambulance to my address. While walking toward the officers, I planned to inform him that I was the victim and that the man on the ground was my ex-husband who violated a court-issued restraining order.

An officer took my copy of the restraining order and read it before passing it over to his partner.

"What happened here tonight, Ms. Henderson?" The officer asked evenly.

I explained to him that my ex-husband knocked on my window around two a.m. wanting to be let in. I informed Mr. Henderson that he was violating a court order and that he needed to leave immediately. We exchanged a few words and then he left. A short time later, I heard a loud bang and then saw Mr. Henderson throwing huge rocks at my truck.

"Why is Mr. Henderson on the ground?"

Now I had a choice to make— lie and say that he fell or tell the truth and inform them that I beat the hell out of Jonathan.

Before I could answer, another officer walked over and whispered several words to his comrade.

"Ms. Henderson you are free to go. A lead detective will be in touch with you within the next twenty-four hours to get your statement for the damage that was done to your vehicle."

The officer who stayed behind pulled me to the side as the ambulance arrived to transport Jonathan to the hospital.

"Mr. Henderson informed us that his injuries are from tripping over one of the large rocks and, since he was under the influence, he lost his balance. That is what's going in my police report and you may want to let the lead detective on this case know that happened" he stated while grinning at me.

'Is this man trying to flirt with me?'

"Off the record ma'am, I had a sister who was a victim of domestic violence. Her aggressor shot her while she was attending her baby shower. She didn't make it, but my niece lived. Sadly, she has permanent damage to her legs. She'll never walk but we are blessed that she is still alive. You did the right thing by getting a restraining order. Anytime he comes around don't fail to call us first. Things could have been worse. We found a loaded gun under the seat of his car. He will be charged for domestic violence and carrying a concealed weapon—one that he is not licensed to have."

The officer must have seen the shock in my eyes because he reassured me that Jonathan would probably have to post a high bail and the judge that he'd have to go before was ruthless. He had no time for ignorance and people who violated the law in his court.

"Thank you so much for your help officer," I said as I shivered at the thought of what could have happened that night. "Things surely could have been worse and one of us could have had a date with the coroner's office."

"You had better get inside ma'am," he said. "It's rather cold outside and you're shaking."

He then walked me to my front door and waited until I had locked it.

It was hard for me to believe what all had happened. I had to spend my Saturday at the dealership having my windows replaced. I had to take out five-hundred dollars from my savings to pay for the deductible. I was saving that cash to take a cruise to the Bahamas in June. Now that incident put a small dent in my spending money. I made a mental note to park my car in the garage from then on.

Before getting back into bed, I made sure that the alarm was set on the house. I grabbed a bottle water from the refrigerator and a bowl of grapes then headed for my bedroom.

'How am I supposed to sleep after all of this?'

I searched for the remote and turned to the Discovery Channel. After setting my alarm clock, I got underneath the blankets and pulled them up to my chin. It wasn't long before sleep overcame me and I was out like a light.

I dreamed that Jonathan was standing over me in my bedroom reaching for my neck. I knew that it was all a dream, but why couldn't I wake up?

Chapter Ten
Who's That Lady?

I spent most of Saturday morning at the dealership that I had purchased my truck from. The very-helpful salesman who assisted me with the purchase of my SUV, walked past me while I was waiting in the reception area.

"Hey Brooke, what brings you in today?" he asked.

"I'm practically having all my windows replaced. A crazed maniac wanted to use my windows as target practice," I said.

"You have to be kidding me," he said. "Do you know who it was?"

"Yes I do," I said. "It was my ex-husband—the lunatic who just doesn't get the hint to leave me alone—did the damage. He came by early this morning in a drunken stupor and thought that he would give me another chance to take him back. He didn't like my response and, as a result, I have close to fifteen-hundred dollars in repairs!"

"Are you using your insurance to cover the repairs?" he asked.

"No, I don't want my premiums to increase so I'll bite the cost and pay for the repairs out of my savings," I said.

"Let me see what I can do to and try to save you a few hundred dollars," he said. "It won't be much, but maybe a little something will help."

When my car was repaired, the friendly salesman came back and announced that he managed to save me twenty percent on my total cost, which was a relief for me. I thanked him as he escorted me to my Navigator that had been vacuumed, cleaned and detailed inside and out.

"Anytime I can help Brooke," he said. "And the pleasure was all mine. After seeing the bright smile on your face, I know my job has been done. Take care and try to enjoy the rest of your weekend."

My truck looked just as good as it did when I drove her off the lot for the first time. It was around noontime and, since it was a gorgeous sunny day, I let the sunroof back and enjoyed the fresh spring air. My stereo was pumping out Impromp2's new hit *"Mocha Soul."*

'The brothers have it going on," I thought to myself as I cruised down I-425 towards the Plaza to pick up my usual Bath and Body products.

I swung my Navigator into a parking spot near the entrance to the mall then clicked the alarm on and headed to the mall entrance. Since it was the middle of the afternoon, there were a lot of people walking from one shop to another.

The Plaza was an upscale strip mall that carried a variety of shops such as The Sharper Image, Barnes and Noble, Victoria's Secret, The Gap, and so many more stores. Restaurants such as The Cheesecake Factory, KC Master Piece and Huston's were a few great places to eat after shopping or to take a for a night on the town. The plaza also had a few jazz bar and grills that had roof-top seating for customers to enjoy while dinning and listening to jazz.

Once I left Bath and Body with my essentials, I headed toward Lane Bryant to pick up a few pairs of underwear and matching bras. I also found a cute lavender negligee and matching robe. As I browsed around the store I saw this to-die-for strapless white dress. Ordinarily white would have not been my first choice, but the way that the dress was cut— it caught my eye. I found my size, took it off the rack and headed for the dressing room to try it on. I admired the way that it fit me. It fit me in such a way that one would have thought I had it tailor made. It had a lettuce-cut edge at the bottom of the dress and slant to one side. The dress was fit around the waist and flowed out from the hips so I didn't have to worry about wearing any body armor. I glanced at the tag and saw the price of the dress was one-hundred and twenty-five dollars. Despite the price and the fact that it wasn't on sale, I made up my mind that I had to have it.

After getting dressed, I took my items to the counter and checked out. The sales woman greeted me with a smile and asked was I able to find everything that I needed? I nodded. She rang up my items, and asked me if I wanted apply for a store charge card. I gave it a thought for a few seconds, and then told her, "No." I wanted to keep a hold of my credit card expenses. To get another charge card would only tempt me to shop more than I needed. As she handed me my packages, she thanked me for shopping at Lane Bryant and handed me a coupon for twenty-five percent off my next purchase. I thanked her and told her to have a nice day and she bid me the same. My feet started barking at me; a true sign that it was time to leave and head home.

As I walked toward my vehicle, I noticed a man who resembled Dante' coming from a cellular store across the street from the parking garage. I spoke with him several days ago and he mentioned that he would be out of town until the weekend. A tall, slim woman was by his side wearing a colorful scarf around her head that covered her hair with glasses to shield her eyes from the sun. The man and his companion were too far away for me to be for sure if it was Dante'. The couple headed for a local department store then disappeared through the front door.

'Why would he lie to me and say that he would be back in town this weekend, only to be back before? I know that Dante' is not my man and he is single and free to do as he pleases, but I don't like to be lied to—no matter what the reason may be.'

I made a mental note to call him on it whenever he called. I didn't have time for head games and would not tolerate being lied to. When it came to Dante', I had slowly let my guard down because I thought that he would be truthful and honest with me. It very well could have not been him, but what was the likelihood of seeing a man who resembled another man almost to the nine?

'That, 'everyone got a twin, crap' ain't working right now! And who was the lady at his side?' I interrogated myself. *'I wonder if she's his ex-fiancé who was desperately trying to get a hold of him since she had something very important to tell him. As far as I'm concerned he's innocent until proven guilty, but three strikes and Brothaman is out!'*

Finally, after walking for what seemed forever, I found my Navigator and clicked my car alarm off before I placed my packages in the back seat. Once the car cooled down, I pulled out the parking garage and headed home to rest my tired, barking and aching feet. I contemplated if I should stop for a pedicure, but, since I had a long day, I decided to pass and turned my car in the direction of home sweet home.

Chapter Eleven
Pleasures of the Night

I was on my way to Dante's house on a late spring evening for a promised night on the town. He finally called to inform me that he was back in town and had actually arrived a few days earlier.

'So it could have very well been Dante' who I saw on the Plaza with his unknown companion.'

I agreed to meet him at his condo around eighty-thirty that night since I had a hectic Saturday and wanted to get some rest before I ventured out for the evening.

After a long, hot shower and a quick do-it-yourself pedicure, I lathered my body with my new Lavender Reign B&B products that I purchased earlier in the day. It had a rich, floral scent that clung to my skin with shimmering flakes of glitter, which made my sun-kissed skin glow and stand out. After pampering my skin and spraying on my favorite scent, I checked myself out. My hair was still fresh from a previous trip to the salon so the only thing that I had to do with it was a quick comb through applying a light coat of oil sheen and hair spray to keep my hairstyle tight.

I put on my newly-purchased black bikini panties and bra set. I removed the straps from the bra to wear with my new strapless dress. I decided to wear a pair of silver high heeled, open-toed shoes. To complete my look, I put on a pair of diamond studs and a silver choker with matching bangles around my wrist. After turning full circle in front of the mirror, I was pleased with how I looked and applied another quick-coat of lip-gloss.

After grabbing my keys and purse from my nightstand, I stepped into the garage and hit the door opener, then set the alarm on the house which gave me sixty seconds to leave.

The sun was just settling over the horizon as I drove toward Dante's condo, which was on the south side of the city. I kept my windows cracked since the temperature dropped a few degrees from the afternoon. The drive to Dante's from where I lived was about thirty minutes.

I arrived at his place a little before eight-thirty since there was very little traffic on the highway and pulled into the parking garage of his building. I had to be buzzed in by Dante' since they had a security door for their exclusive residents who dished out a whopping quarter-of-a-million for their lavish digs. I was impressed at the entrance that was complete with a twenty-four hour doorman who greeted all visitors with the tip of his hat and a warm, friendly smile. After walking through the grand foyer complete with marbled floors and gold fixtures, I pressed the button for the elevator to take me to Dante's floor. As the elevator neared his floor, I could hear smooth jazz emitting from his surround-sound stereo, and I smelled the scent of jasmine floating throughout the air.

When the door opened to his floor, Dante' was standing at the entrance with an array of colorful flowers wrapped in a huge red bow.

"Hello, baby girl," he said and took my hand to lead me into his living room. "These are for you."

He then kissed me deep and slowly. I managed to gather myself and thanked him for the beautiful flowers as he led me to the couch to get comfortable.

"It's good to see you again, Brooke, I was thinking about you the entire time that I was out of town. I couldn't concentrate during my meetings and I wanted desperately, to call you at every chance I got.

"I was wrapped up in meetings for hours on end with a prospective client who will be signing with my record label. My business partner and I ended our business meeting early and we both decided to leave a little earlier than planned. I got back into town late last night and did some shopping and errands earlier today."

On that note, I took my cue to ask him if he was shopping on the Plaza today.

"As a matter of fact, I was around noontime," he replied while looking up at the sky as if his past activities were planted on his ceiling.

I told him that I thought I saw him and a lady walking into a department store.

"I wasn't sure," I said. "Since you had company, I didn't think that is was a good thing to walk towards you."

"Yes, that was my ex-fiancé, and I you saw. I finally agreed to meet with her," he said.

I started to feel heat coming from my ears and said to myself, *'Damn not again, Brooke!'*

I hated being played and I refused to play reindeer games with any man ever again. He must have read my thoughts by the frown and narrowing of my eyes.

"Now wait a minute, baby girl, before you draw the wrong conclusion, my ex would not stop harassing me until I agreed to meet with her. She had something important to discuss with me. Since I was running errands, meeting her in public was a good decision. I did not want that chick back inside my pad for a damn thing."

"Did she ever get around to what was so important that she had to tell you?" I asked.

"No, she tried to play me by stalling and beating around the bush. She wasted her time and mines by saying that she was sorry for what she done and realized the error of her ways. She was practically on her hands and knees begging me to take her back and to give her another chance. It was to the point that she was making a scene and I had to lead her out of the store. She informed me that she broke up with her boy toy."

"Why," I asked if I gave one cent.

"He was abusive. Plus, he was angry with her for getting his ass whipped by me on the night that I caught them in bed together.

"She went as far as to say that she realized that I was the best thing that happened to her. She wanted another chance to prove to me that she had changed and never stopped loving me. I wasn't feeling any of it and told her that there wasn't a snowball's chance in a cool hell that she and I were getting back together ever again.

"That's when the same woman, who I knew was a drama queen, showed her true colors. I was called every name except the one that my momma gave me. She threatened that she was going to make my life hell on earth, and blah, blah, blah. She got nose-to-nose with me and I had to back up several times to avoid being smacked by her. She pushed all my buttons, even slapped me in my face several times. I was raised not to hit women by my mom and had to restrain her several times. Enough was enough; I left her standing there on the corner screaming like a stark-raving lunatic. She blew up my cell phone and left several threatening messages on my voice mail.

"I've instructed the doorman that, under no circumstances, is she allowed on the premises. Monday, I will be downtown, first thing, to file a restraining order against sister girl. It's been crazy for most of the afternoon and I didn't want her to get the best of me. That's why I called to take you out— to help forget about the day's events. I wanted to spend my evening with someone who makes me smile."

Man did I feel stupid for jumping to conclusions before Dante' had a chance to tell me what happened. I apologized to him and told him that I assumed the worst when I saw him with another woman.

"I know that you're not my man, but I do find something special with you and was only protecting my feelings before I would get hurt," I said.

He sat beside me and placed his hand below my chin and said, "Look, baby girl, my intentions are not to hurt you; only to treat you like you deserved to be treated—as a Queen. I know you've been through some difficult times with your ex-husband and my only desire is to make you happy and to take away those bad memories."

He then took the bouquet of flowers from my hand and placed them on his living room table and helped me to my feet. He pulled me closer to him and wrapped his arms around my waist. I tilted my head upward and gazed into his eyes as we both leaned closer so our lips could touch. He slowly kissed me on the corners of my lips then worked his way to the side of my neck. He then whispered in my ear that I smelled like heaven while rubbing the lower part of my back.

He worked his way back to my lips and began to passionately kiss me, which made me feel light-headed and dizzy. Our kissing began to ignite a desire within my secret place that had been on lock-down for months. Since we were standing so close to one another, I could feel his friend grow and harden right on me. One of his hands reached to caress my breast while the other grabbed and squeezed a handful of my behind. He then pulled the top down from my dress and began to gently suck on my ridged nipples. I arched my back and moaned with pleasure as the heat intensified and flourished like a flower in bloom. Dante' then slipped his hand underneath my dress and reached towards the band of my panties and rubbed his finger tips on the opening of my pleasure zone. That sent another round of chills down my arms and spine. He worked his fingers deeper and moved in a slow rhythmic motion. With each thrust, my breath quickened and I began to pant and moan louder as he pleased me and made me quiver in ecstasy.

From deep within, a force so powerful erupted like a volcano and made my knees buckle from the intensity of the orgasm that flowed free with splendor. He held me closer while he brought me endless stimulation that seemed to last forever.

"That's right baby girl, let it go," Dante' said and kissed me ever-so-softly as I gently came down from my high. I looked him in the eye with amazement and awe. He helped me adjust my dress and gather myself.

"That's just a sample of what I have to offer to you, and what gives you pleasure does the same for me in return." He kissed me once more and smiled at the way I swayed from side to side to gather control of myself. The phone rang and Dante' hit the speaker button and said, "Hello."

"Mr. Hunter, your car is now around front."

"Thank you, Brent, I'll be down in a few minutes."

Before heading down, I asked him where his bathroom was. He took my hand and led me down the hallway.

"Everything is there that you may need and I can get you anything that isn't there," he said.

After using the bathroom and freshening up, I then touched up my makeup and smoothed out the hem of my dress. The boy was good— not a hair out of place. I also noticed a new glow emitting from my cheeks.

As I approached the living room, I saw that Dante' had made the final preparations to leave.

"Are you ready, Ms. Lady?" he asked.

"Yes, I'm ready."

He led the way to his front door. We made it down to the lobby and the doorman, Brent, held the door to Dante's awaiting Escalade open for the both of us. After opening the passenger door for me, the valet driver wished both Dante' and I a good evening. I was curious as to where we would be going, and was taken by surprise to see that we were going to dine at Club Phoenix, which was located in the Jazz and Blues district of 18th and Vine.

As we pulled up to Club Phoenix, we noticed that there was a line of people waiting to enter. To my surprise, Rachelle Farrell was the evening's performer. I looked over toward Dante' and noticed that he had a huge grin on his face. He started to chuckle.

"Surprise, baby girl!" he said.

"I know how much you love Rachelle. I managed to get VIP tickets for tonight's performance."

I squealed with laughter and told him that I was pleasantly surprised and knew that we were going to have a great time.

We pulled up to the valet and Dante' got out and came over to my side of the vehicle. He took my hand as I stepped down from the Escalade and headed towards the entrance. The crowd was eagerly waiting to go inside of the club. Dante' gave the doorman the VIP passes and he stamped our tickets then handed them back to him along with two blue wrist bands.

Club Phoenix was almost filled to capacity and many of the good seats by the stage were taken. Dante' saw a few of his friends and their dates as we walked toward the VIP section. He introduced me to his friends and we exchanged greetings before being seated. A waiter came over and took our drink orders. Dante's business partner and best friend, Rome, came to our table with a lovely, slender mocha-colored sister clinging to his arm like skin.

"What's up man? What you know good?" Rome asked.

"You man, you is what's going down Dante'," said and then does the "Brothaman" handshake and hug thing. Rome looked over my way and asked how I was doing.

"It's nice to finally meet you in person, Brooke. I remember seeing you on the day that my boy had his fender bender."

"Oh yes, I remember you!" I said. "You and Dante' had the poor man afraid for his life."

"Can you believe how fast dude ran down that ramp? I saw smoke coming from his heels he was running so fast," he said while shaking his head from the memory of that day. We continued the conversation until the lights dimmed and the show began.

Rachelle entered the stage wearing a long white flowing skirt with a matching sheer blouse and a black tank top underneath. Her hair was styled with kinky twists, which framed her face beautifully. Her skin was completely flawless and had a rich glow to it. She was striking and her performance was phenomenal. She performed some of my favorite songs and she ended the show with a bang.

Afterwards, she came to the VIP section. I was pleasantly surprised that she stopped by our table first and greeted us with a warm, "Hello."

I tried my best to keep my jaw from hanging and told her how much I enjoyed her show. She said that she was glad that she had the opportunity to perform for such a valiant crowd and planned to make Club Phoenix one of her performance hot spots.

She spoke with Dante' for awhile and exchanged contact information to talk about a possible recording session with the new artist that he signed to his record label earlier in the week. Before leaving, she handed Rome's date and myself an autographed picture and bid us a great evening. I was smiling so hard that I thought the corners of my lips would crack.

"Did you enjoy the show, baby girl?" Dante' asked.

"Boy did I. I can't believe that Rachelle came over to our table and spoke with us. She had such a kindred spirit about her, and her voice is as smooth as silk."

"I'm glad that you enjoyed yourself and had a great time," he said while leaning over to give me a hug.

We stayed for another hour and then said our goodbyes to Rome and his date. We waited while the valet pulled Dante's ride curbside and then headed back to his pad so he could drop me off to my car.

After arriving at his place shortly after one a.m., he walked me to my vehicle. I deactivated the alarm and put my purse on the passenger side before I reached to give Dante' a hug and a soft, gentle kiss on the lips.

"Thank you once again for a wonderful evening," I said. "I'll never forget this. I had the chance to see one of my favorite artists *and* get an autographed photo of her, too! This was the icing on the cake for me."

"I aim to please, baby girl, and I am glad that you had such a good time. Be sure to call me when you get home and let me know that you made it in safely."

"I sure will," I said, hugging him once more before stepping into my vehicle. He stood there until I backed up from the parking spot and then buzzed the gate to let me out.

As I was pulling out, a car flew by me. I had to brake and turn sharply in order to avoid a collision. I honked my horn and my head in disbelief at how fast the car was traveling. It turned at the corner at break-neck speed.

After regaining my composure, I continued the drive home.

"I guess they give anyone a driver's license these days," I said out loud.

I was exhausted and had to roll down my window to let the cool air keep me awake. Several minutes later, I pulled into my driveway and hit the garage door button above my visor, patiently waiting for the door to rise. I had a spacious garage that could comfortably park two large vehicles with enough space for storage and miscellaneous garden and yard equipment.

After pulling in, I pressed the button for the door to come down as I gathered my purse and keys. I wondered why the door took forever and a day to go close, but still wait safely in my ride until it was completely down.

I loved the fact that I could go directly from my garage through the kitchen door and then into my home after deactivating the alarm.

I undressed quickly and took a quick shower to help me relax and ready myself for bed while reflecting over the night's event. Dante' scored major points for surprising me and redeemed himself in the process. I could still feel his fingers tenderly pleasing and giving me pure pleasure. I made a mental note to call and thank him, once again, for the wonderful evening after setting my alarm for an early rise. I wanted to hit the gym and do my groceries shopping early so that I could have most of my Saturday free to catch up on some much-needed house work.

It wasn't long after sleep overtook me as I'm nestled deep within my comforter and fluffy goose-down pillows. I was so tired that even a four-alarm fire could not wake me from my deep slumber. Without my knowledge, the car that blew past me as I left Dante's condo was parked across from my house watching and waiting for any sign of life. As the dawn rose, a neighbor would later inform the police that she noticed the car with dark tinted windows sit idle as she took her Maltese for his morning walk. She thought it strange and wondered who would leave their parked car running at that time of the morning.

Some weeks later, drifters would find it abandoned with a body charred beyond recognition in the trunk on the opposite end of town.

Chapter Twelve
911

My mom called my cell phone after not being able to reach me on the office phone. I knew that it was important because, usually when she couldn't reach me, she would leave a message. So, when I saw her number show up on the caller ID, I was immediately worried.

"What's wrong, mom?" I asked as my heart began to beat faster by the minute.

"It's Fred. He's fallen again and I'm on my way to the hospital."

Before I knew it, I was grabbing my keys and purse and practically running to the garage while still on the phone.

"What hospital is he being taken to?"

"I've already called his doctors and they want to meet me at North Hospital as soon as possible."

"Stay put, mom. I'll swing by to pick you up and take you since you are in no shape to drive.

"Okay, but hurry dear. I'm a nervous wreck and my hands are shaking badly."

Fred was my step-dad of fourteen years who suffered from various aliments due to having diabetes. He had the disease since he was nineteen. He found out after enlisting in the Army. For most of his life, Fred had to take care of other family members. He saw two other siblings battle diabetes to only succumb to its side effects. He fought a long and hard battle and refused to give up even though he was facing amputation of part of his right foot. Since he had no feeling in his legs, it was hard for him to feel a cut or scratch, leaving him prone to infection and other ailments. Still, I had to admit that Fred was a trooper! He hadn't let diabetes get the best of him, yet.

I arrived at their house within ten minutes of my mother's phone call and honked my horn for her to come out.

"Hey baby," she said and gave me a quick peck on the check.

"What happened this time?" I asked her.

"I was helping him get dressed for his dialysis appointment and, while he was standing, he began to shake and had a blank stare on his face. Before I knew it, he collapsed to the floor and started to convulse uncontrollably. The EMT thinks that he's had a diabetic-seizure. He thinks that the worst is over since Fred was responding well to his questions when they took him to the hospital on the ambulance.

"That's good news to hear, mom." I said while en route to the hospital.

We arrived at the emergency room just as the medics were wheeling Fred in. His doctor was already there and was waiting patiently by the nurse's station as my mother and I frantically approached him. After greeting us, Dr. Hautin informed us that he had spoken with the EMT and also thought that Fred had suffered a diabetic seizure.

"I cannot be for sure until we conduct an MRI and get him stable," Dr. Hautin said. "We'll, more than likely, keep him for several days for observation and administer medication to him through an IV to control his seizures and treat him with medication after he's released. After I assess him, you both will be able to come back and see him. I'll come and get you after my assessment is done, which should take about twenty minutes or so."

We thanked him and walked over to the waiting room. I grabbed two cups of coffee and some muffins for mom and I to help settle our nerves.

As we were waiting, I called my office and informed Shelia, my secretary, that I had an emergency and wouldn't be coming back for the rest of the day. I let her know to direct all calls to my voice mail and that I'd check them when I get home that evening. She told me that she would be praying for my step-dad to have a speedy recovery. I thanked her and, after giving her several additional instructions, ended the call.

It took awhile but Dr. Hautin finally came out to inform us that Fred was stable and resting and that we could go to his room and visit with him. He also informed us that the test confirmed Fred did suffer a diabetic seizure and, with medication, could be treated.

The doctor wanted to monitor his blood sugar levels closely as they might have been a contributing factor to the seizures. He thought that Fred was taking too much insulin after checking his blood sugar levels, which were reading extremely high. My mother confirmed the fact that Fred would check his blood sugar after eating or drinking something with sugar in it, which may have given him a false reading. She tried to keep a handle on those things but, sometimes, Fred might not have been at home and would check his blood sugar with the kit that he kept inside of his truck.

I'd spoken with Fred about the importance of him keeping track of his insulin intake and being sure to chart and monitor all of his readings. My mother reassured Dr. Hautin that she would make sure that he stuck to his daily schedule to prevent this from reoccurring. We both thanked him and headed in the direction of Fred's room.

We could hear Fred's voice down the hallway as we neared his room. He was telling a nurse that he could use the restroom by himself and that he didn't need her help. The nurse was persistent and told Fred that he was a fall risk and she had to watch him while he used the restroom.

Fred's four-word reply, "Like hell you are" cracked me up. My mom nudged me on my right side and told me to behave.

I tried to put a straight face on as we entered the room but erupted with laughter as Fred snatched the back of his gown. Fred looked toward mom and I as we entered the room and took the opportunity to tell the nurse that he would call her when he was ready to go to the restroom.

He had an *"I'm not going to give up the battle because no one's going to see me naked but my wife"* look on his face.

The nurse, who was completely flustered and red in the cheeks, said, "Well Mr. Flowers, you cannot go unassisted. Maybe your wife can talk some sense into you."

I had to pinch myself to keep from interrupting with more laughter. After the nurse left, Fred's face lit up.

"Hey, foxy Lady," he said.

My mom gave him a look of disapproval and shook her head saying; "You know she was only trying to help."

"I know, honey, but nobody will see my goodness except for you!"

He then playfully sang, *"My goodies, my goodies, not my goodies."*

At that last comment, I couldn't help myself— I let it all loose. I laughed so hard I used stomach muscles I didn't know I had. No sooner than I stopped laughing, I looked over to Fred and started laughing all over again. My mom started in with laughter and Fred tried to act innocent like he wasn't the cause of me having side-splitting laughter.

I gained control of myself and drank a cup of water to control my hiccups. Mom took a seat near Fred's bed and I sat near the window on a bench seat. My mom stressed to Fred the seriousness of how bad the seizure was and that he needed to be very careful about how he took his insulin and his daily monitoring. He promised to be mindful of his medications and reassured mom that he wouldn't let it get out of control, again. Mom reached over and gave him a big kiss on the lips and pinched him to let him know that she wasn't playing.

"I know foxy; you don't have to worry about a thing."

I sighed and realized how much they both loved one another.

'When I grow up, I want to find a love like theirs.' As mom helped him to the restroom, Fred said, "When can I blow this gig?"

I started laughing all over again until I couldn't laugh any longer.

Chapter Thirteen
Rain, Go Away

It had been a month since my step-dad's short stay in the hospital, which brought forth significant changes in his health care and eating habits. He promised, both my mom and I, that he would stick to his word. So far, he had not disappointed us.

Fall had just begun with leaves changing colors and cooler temperatures that created light jacket-wearing weather.

On one particularly cold and dreary Saturday afternoon, I was cuddled up in my favorite winged-back chaise lounge that sat directly in front of my bedroom window. I'd lit several candles, which emitted the smell of jasmine to create a mellow and relaxing mood in my bedroom while also giving my bedroom subtle lighting.

Sitting on my night table beside the lounge was a glass of red wine and my latest Eric Jerome Dickey novel that had been left untouched for too long. I was in a somber mood for no reason to speak of and had not felt like doing much that day.

My friend, Gabby, called to see if I wanted to go to the mall to do some shopping and have a late afternoon lunch but I told her to give me a rain check. I had to catch up on some paperwork that was left undone from the previous week. I heard her smacking her lips on the phone, chewing on her favorite snack—fruit trail mix. The girl was always eating on something and never gained an ounce. I was thinking I should force-feed her a whole cherry cheesecake with whipped topping. If I even thought too hard about eating a slice of cheesecake, I gained five pounds on *each* of my thighs.

I told Gabby that I'd get back with her later on in the week and, no sooner than I hung up, my phone rang again.

"Hello?" I said to the caller on the line. "Hello?" There was no answer. I looked at the caller ID to see who was calling and it showed private. I could tell that someone was there because I could hear breathing in the background.

After several seconds, I pushed the "End" button and dialed the code to block whoever had called me from a private line.

"That will take care of them," I spat out.

I had to remind myself to add on the feature to my phone that prevented private calls from coming through.

When I finally managed to pick up my book to read, it was well into the afternoon. The rain still hadn't let up and it was beginning to thunder while lightning danced across the sky.

I tried hard to focus on my novel that I was reading but, as I read along, my eyes grew heavier with sleep and —before I knew it— I was out for the count until something fell to the floor, which startled me awake. I jumped and yelped like a dog with its tail caught in a door. I heard myself asking "Who's there?" before I realized that my book had fallen to the floor.

I breathed a quick sigh of relief and glanced at the clock on the DVD player to find that it was well after ten o'clock.

'Wow, I must have been more tired than I realized to have slept for so long and without eating the entire afternoon.'

I was slightly woozy as I stood to close my blinds and curtains in my bedroom.

When I reached over to pull the cord down on my mini-blinds, I saw a dark figure cloaked in black standing just below my window seal. As I took a couple of steps back, I gasped with surprise and managed to stumble into something which made me scream because I thought it was someone standing behind me. I swung around quickly and delivered a quick jab-punch-kick into the bedpost that stood about six feet tall. After realizing that I'd just done a Bruce Lee move on my bed, I gathered myself and instinctively reached for my cordless phone, then blew the candles out that were illuminating my bedroom.

I tip-toed to my window to see that whoever was standing outside was no longer peeping into my bedroom and, hopefully, was well on their way after being discovered by me. Now I was facing the dilemma as to whether to call the police or stay up all night with a baseball bat resting against my chest.

My best bet was to call the police and have them take a look around my property to see if the person outside my window tried to gain entry into my house. As I was about to dial 911, I heard a loud bang from the back of my house near the kitchen. I quickly dialed 911 and told them what happened and that I thought that someone was trying to break into my home.

It was when I heard another loud bang at the back of my house that I know I needed a little more protection than just a baseball bat. I opened my jewelry box and retrieved the small silver key hidden inside a panel that opened the locked box I kept underneath the head of my bed. Inside was a silver, nickel-plated 25-caliber Smith & Wesson handgun that I purchased shortly after the Jonathan incident a few weeks ago. I inserted a bullet into the chamber and quickly loaded the clip with the remaining nine bullets.

I tried to steady my hands as I inserted the clip into the handgun because I could hear whoever outside trying to gain entry into my home. After several seconds, I got the clip in and disengaged the safety then quickly closed and locked my bedroom door. I was sitting in the dark so my eyes had to adjust to not having any light.

The assailant started kicking at my back door.

'Dagnabbit, what is taking the police so long to get here?' I asked myself as I dialed Dante's cell phone only to get his voicemail after the second ring.

I saw that I might have to go at it alone and so I steadied myself and tried not to be so afraid of what was about to come.

From a distance, I could hear sirens and prayed that it was the police on the way. The next sound that I heard chilled my blood starting from my head to my toes. After the last major blow to my back door, I heard it splinter against the force of the many blows that it endured. My back door bounced against the wall so fiercely that it shook the front two windows of my home. For several seconds after, there was complete silence and I wondered where the intruder was or if they were searching for me room to room

I had a three-bedroom two-bath ranch-style home and, since my bedroom sat in the front of the house, people had to pass the other bedrooms to reach mine. I knew that might buy me some time to prepare to defend myself — no matter the cost.

Since I had hardwood floors, I could hear a chair from my dining room table being pushed to the side and could judge the distance of the intruder. I stood on the far side of my armoire to give myself some sort of shield and took a stance just in case I had recoil when I fired the gun.

My mother always told me to shoot first and ask questions later so that was exactly what I was prepared to do. The floorboard near the hall that separated the bedroom creaked against the weight of being walked on and, at the point, I was really scared and afraid for my life.

My heart was beating a thousand times a minute and I could only think about how the hell I was going to go against an unknown assailant who seemed to be out to seek and destroy.

Being married to Jonathan had taught me a thing or two about defending myself. We had a turbulent and volatile marriage in which many arguments led to knock 'em down fights. I promised, somebody was going to get their behind kicked one way or another.

I learned to always be prepared and never turn a back on someone who meant to do harm. I could remember the one and only time that I turned my back on Jonathan after a huge argument. I turned my back from him and walked away. He tapped me on my shoulder and, before I knew it, *wham!*

The fool hit me closed-fist in the mouth and split my lip in three different places. I still carried the scar to remind me of the argument turned into a fight gone wrong. And, the sad thing is, he still said that I provoked him into hitting me and, if I had agreed with him, then none of it would have happened.

'Yeah right and I believe that cows fly and monkeys can drive.'

The doorknob rattling brought me back to my current reality. I could hear the knob being jiggled from side to side as the assailant tried to get into my room.

"Brooke, stay focused," I whispered to myself softly while steadying the gun and locking my elbows to brace for the recoil. My bedroom door shook as it was bumped upon. That's when I also heard the police sirens, which stopped directly in front of my home.

The door was bumped so violently that it cracked. Instinctively, I fired off a shot towards the top of the door. The recoil jerked me a few steps backward. I regained my stance, quickly, then raised my arms again ready to fire if needed.

"Ma'am don't shoot!" I heard a voice say outside my bedroom door. It was the police.

"Put your weapon down and open the door."

I was hesitant to comply because I didn't know if it was the intruder or really the police outside my door so I yelled back, "Prove it!"

The voice on the other side of my door said, "I'll have the 911 dispatcher to call you and verify that, indeed, there is an officer who is here to assist you."

Several seconds later, my telephone rang and I looked at the caller I.D. to see that the call was from the police department. I answered after the third ring.

"Yes," I said to the caller on the other end of the phone.

"Ma'am this is a dispatcher from the police department calling to inform you that an officer is there to assist you with your emergency. You have to put down your weapon and open the door in order for them to assist you and do their job," she calmly stated.

So there was, in fact, a police officer at my door and not the assailant who kicked in my back door.

"I'll stay on the phone with you until the officer has made sure that you're okay and secured your home."

I was so nervous that I didn't realize how badly my hands were shaking until I tried to unlock my bedroom door. After several tries, I finally managed to unlock the door to an officer pointing a gun directly at my chest.

"Ma'am, where is your weapon?" the officer asked. I pointed to the nightstand and told him that the safety was engaged. He looked over to see if I was telling the truth and ordered me to sit down on the chaise lounge.

The dispatcher asked if I was still there and if I was all right. I let her know that I was okay and that the officer was in the room with me. She then asked me to speak with the officer, so I handed him the telephone.

After several minutes passed, he conveyed several codes and then wrote a case number down on his note pad.

After ending the call and handing me the phone, he asked if I was okay.

I breathed a sigh of relief and nodded my head. He noticed that I was visibly shaken and asked if he needed to call an ambulance to check me over. I told him that it was not necessary and that I was just frightened and somewhat nervous.

He then two-wayed his partner and informed him that the premises were secured. After several minutes, his partner, who I recognized as being the arresting officer who carted Jonathan off to jail several weeks ago, arrived.

"Good evening Ms. Henderson. Are you okay?" he asked.

I reassured him that I was fine— just shaken and that I needed some water to quench my thirst.

"I can get if for you," he said. "I can see that you're in no shape to stand at the moment."

I told him that I had some bottled water in the refrigerator and that there was enough if he and his partner would like some. He thanked me for my hospitality and headed in the direction of my kitchen.

The remaining officer then asked me if it was all right that he take me to the main headquarters to answer some questions with the detective who would be assigned to my case.

First, I wanted to know if the officers caught who broke into my home. I shuddered once more at the thought of what could have happened, had not the police arrived in time. The officer stated that the suspect was nowhere to be found. Whoever it was, was well on their way upon hearing the police's sirens.

"Great, then some nut case is still out there," I said.

"Unfortunately, yes. You may want to invest in an alarm system with a control pad at several key areas in your house. I suggest one by your front door, garage and kitchen entry, and in your bedroom. Just in case an emergency should arise like this again, the security monitors can quickly alert the police."

I made a mental note to do exactly what the officer suggested first thing in the morning.

"What about my back door?" I asked.

I had to make sure that my home was secure before I left.

"Can you give me some time in order to call my step-dad and a locksmith out to repair the locks on my door?"

He gave me the okay to call the necessary people out to fix my door.

"I have to take your gun with me and make sure that it's properly registered," he said. "This is procedure only and you'll get it back as soon as the registration on it clears."

"How long does that take?"

"Usually within forty-eight hours you can pick it up from the sheriff's department located in the lower level of police headquarters," he said.

I let out a long sigh because the events of the night were overwhelming.

I heard a knock on my front door, and the officer questioning me asked if I wanted him to answer it.

I nodded and he said that he'd be right back.

Before leaving my room, he asked: "Are you sure you're up for all this?"

I told him for now, but that I was really shaken and scared to be alone. He looked at the bullet hole above my bedroom door and said, "Whoever was outside of your house should be more afraid of you."

At that comment we both released a much-needed laugh.

"Just call me Annie Oakley!" I said which made him laugh even more.

Then he said, "In all seriousness ma'am, you have to be careful. Contrary to what people may believe, it's not okay to shoot first and ask questions later. You have to be really careful because the consequences can be deadly and you don't want to spend the rest of your life with guilt. Just be more careful."

He smiled before turning to go into the living room.

I heard my step-dad in the living room asking the officer "What the hell was going on?"

I yelled out to him from my bedroom to let him know that I was okay.

"Are you sure everything is all right?" he asked coming into my bedroom.

"Yes, I'm fine," I answered reassured to see him. "I'll come out once I get off the phone from talking to the locksmith."

"Okay, well I'm going to check out the back door and see what it is that I need to do while you're on the phone," Fred said leaving my room.

I could hear the officers and Fred conversing back and forth about who he thought may have wanted to do harm to me. The first thing that came out of Fred's mouth was, "That black-ass fool who she used to be married to. That no-good son of a bitch has been trouble since day one and I have a notion to haul off and put my foot off in his ass just for GP!" he said.

I'm cracking up inside because, despite being saved, Fred would say whatever was on his mind no matter what. I knew that he only had my best interest at heart and that my safety was first.

The locksmith said that he could be at my home in about an hour, but stated that there would be an extra fifty-dollar charge because it was after hours.

Despite my better judgment, I agreed to it because I did not want to leave my house unprotected while I was downtown speaking with the detective. After hanging up from him, I went into the kitchen to survey the damage. When I saw my back door buckled in, my jaw hit the ground. The frame had completely splintered along the edges and the door handle was lying on the ground. Fred was taking measurements and stopped to look at me when I didn't say anything.

"Are you okay, Bucket?" he asked again using my childhood nickname because I would always carry a bucket around with me that was filled with my favorite toys.

"I guess, I'm just in awe at how much damage was done," I said. "Whoever was outside of my house must have really wanted to get in and hurt me."

"Don't worry Bucket," Fred said. "I'll have everything better than new in a couple of hours. I am putting a reinforced door made of steel on here so the frame will be sturdy and will not buckle under pressure. I'd like to see someone try to kick it in!"

Fred must have seen the look of shock on my face because he put his hammer down and came over to me giving me a big hug.

"It's all right," he said. "You know that I'll make sure that nothing will ever happen to you."

"I know, Fred. I guess I'm just taking it all in and wondering who would to do this? I am shocked and asking myself whether it was a random act or was it done purposely."

Fred looked around the room to see if the police there were listening and leaned in and said, "Make sure that you're always protected and, if need be, don't be afraid to pop a bullet into someone's ass."

I let out a burst of laughter after that comment.

"You're a mess."

"I know, but I'm serious Bucket. Don't be afraid to use it if need be okay?"

"All right. I promise to protect myself no matter what the cost."

"I told your mom that I would spend a few nights propped on your couch with the shotgun in hand if you need me to."

"I'll be okay," I reassured him and gave him a big hug and then thanked him for always being there for me.

"Not a problem, Bucket," he said with a wink of his eye. "You know you're like my own, and we are partners in crime."

The officers then came into the kitchen and asked if I was ready to leave. I told him that I had to grab my purse and keys and then I would be ready. Fred told me that he would stay until I got back and that my mom would stop by later on the next day to bring us lunch. I said goodbye and the officer led me to his patrol car. He asked me, once more, if I was doing all right. I told him that I was fine.

I was in total silence all the way down to the police headquarters. I could tell from the looks of it that it was going to be a long and eventful day.

Chapter Fourteen
The Meeting

Mr. Billings was in my office with the two clients who I recently assigned attorneys. He was going over all the expectations with the clients in a joint meeting— nothing pertaining to their case, but simply telling them that they could lie to their own selves or their family but not to us or the courts. We worked out with each client that they would pay a flat-fee of five-hundred dollars for our services. Our interns, LaTonya Hutton and Andrea Hillsworth, were eager and listening attentively. Both interns graduated as valedictorians from their schools and had many honors and accomplishments to place on future resumes.

LaTonya was offered a full scholarship at Hampton University while Andrea was offered a partial one at Berkley University. Andrea wanted to study malpractice law while LaTonya wanted to specialize in Corporate Law. I could tell that both students were purpose-driven and were determined to accomplish the goals that they had set for themselves. Their attorneys should have no problem with those two bright and talented women beside them.

Mr. Billings rambled on with a speech that I knew all too well. He used the same one each time we took on a new case. For all that mattered, I could recite the speech in my sleep. He went on to tell the clients how lucky they were to be chosen to receive our services. He stated that we had cases backed up as long as the Mississippi. At that comment, I rolled my eyes to the back of my head and muttered under my breath that he was full of it. I didn't think that man knew how irritating his speeches were and that no one really listened to them but himself. The clients just smiled and went along with his dry tail. With free legal help for cases that could run in the thousands, I'd be all ears, too.

Finally, after what seemed like forever, he asked me to show the interns to where they would be working. Before I did so, he wanted a brief word with me. I asked LaTonya and Andrea to have a seat out in the waiting area just outside of my office as our clients also left my office heading towards the lobby. Mr. Billings patiently waited then, no sooner than the door closed, he swung around and glared at me.

I said, "Is there a problem"?

"As a matter of fact, there is," he said while making himself comfortable in my office chair.

I stared at him in disbelief thinking, '*the nerve of him.*'

I received a call several days ago from Mr. Dalton, who was Mr. Billings' supervisor. Mr. Dalton made it obvious that he didn't care for Mr. Billings whatsoever.

"I do not appreciate you going over my head with the issues regarding the internship program. I thought that I made it clear with my position on that issue, Ms. Henderson.

"I got chewed out as a result of your little phone call, and, the next time that happens, you will answer to me. If that ever happens again, you and I will have a serious problem," he said.

Now I'm thinking to myself that the little dwarf from Oz had some nerve. What he failed to realize was that I didn't answer to him in any capacity

I chanted to myself and closed my eyes several seconds before I gave him a response. To challenge his authority, I called him by his first name.

"Roger, you are sorely mistaken in thinking that I have to run anything by you, first of all," I said. "Secondly, if you thought that I was going to stand here and let you throw your *so-called* weight around, you have another thing coming!"

I was not the one and I refused to let him ruin my day. My first instinct was to flick the little dwarf out of my office by his big ears and tell him to go find the Yellow Brick Road, but I kept my cool. I walked around to my desk where he was sitting and then stooped down eye level to him. I was so close to him that I could smell his hot dragon-manure smelling breath. However, I didn't let that distract me. I had a point to get across.

"Listen, little man, you are not my supervisor and I'm not intimidated by you in the least bit. If you ever disrespect me again, there will be a high price to pay. I'm not going to have you speaking to me as if I belong in a special class," I told him.

Mr. Billings became flushed in the face and turned beet red. He started stuttering and coughing like he swallowed a cow bone and immediately jumped up from my seat tripping over his own two feet. He finally managed to catch his breath and stepped away from my desk; never taking his eyes off me. I then took a couple of tissues from my desk to wipe the spit that he left after almost choking to death.

'Yuck, the man is so gross and has no manners, whatsoever.'

He managed to gain his composure and went on to say that he was not afraid of the likes of me and that he would do whatever he saw fit in order to comply with the guidelines of the open-access client program.

I placed my hands on my hips and said, "If you're not afraid of me, Mr. Billings, then why are your hands shaking? I don't issue any threats—I make promises! I'll do whatever I see fit in order for this program to continue to serving low-income people or families. Legal help is just as necessary as medical help. Without either one, you are screwed!"

"Well, we'll just have to see about that," he said practically running into the office door. He fumbled with the doorknob before finally letting himself out.

I flopped down in my seat and laughed so hard it felt like I could've passed out. I stopped laughing and then would envision him running into the door and start to laugh all over again. I heard a knock at my office door, which was the only reason that I stopped laughing.

"Come in," I said.

Shelia, my secretary, stuck her hand inside the door waving a white tissue, then asked if the coast was clear.

"Come on in, girl," I replied. "It's all right."

She came in and sat in a chair on the other side of my desk.

"What did you do to poor old Billings?" she asked. "Who me? I wouldn't hurt a fly much less Mr. Billings," I said with a sly grin.

"Sure, yeah right! I'm Boo-Boo, last name is Da' Fool!" she said followed by a round of laughter from the both of us.

"Mr. Billings has had issues with me from day one, especially since I beat him out for the position that I'm in now. He thinks that he can interject with any decisions that I make and I'm supposed to just step back and let him do it. Not going to happen in this lifetime or the next," I said with much attitude.

"I know that's right. Don't let him stress you out. He ran to the elevator so fast, I thought that his butt was on fire and he was trying to put it out," Shelia said.

"Well, I just know this: Mr. Billings thinks that whatever he says is the golden rule," I said. "He wants to be more than what he is so badly that he will try to intimidate anybody who might stand in his way. I was born at night but not last night, and you have to get up pretty early to try and pull wool over my eyes."

We both high-fived each other after the last comment and started to laugh again.

"Well, I originally came in here to let you know that I was going to lunch and wanted to know if I could get you anything," Shelia said.

I asked her to get me whatever she was having with large bottled water if she didn't mind. I reached for my purse to pay her and she said that it was her treat. I asked her if she was sure, and she said yes. She also told me that she sent LaTonya and Andrea on an hour lunch break and instructed then to wait in the employee conference room, read their handbooks and fill out other demographic sheets, along with contact info. I thanked her and I told her that I didn't know what I would do if I didn't have her assistance.

"Not a problem, girlfriend," she said. "You know you took care of me when I needed time off to deal with my ex-husband and the custody battle that we had with my kids. I will always be indebted to you for being a great boss and a good friend."

"Go on to lunch girl before our fly make-up gets messed up, and you know that wouldn't be a pretty sight with mascara running down our faces."

That made her smile as she got up to leave.

After she closed the door, I looked at my office phone and noticed that my call notes light was blinking. I must have missed the call when I was giving Mr. Billings the what for.

I picked up the phone and hit the blinking light that directed me to my call notes. The automated voice stated that I had one new message and then gave me the time and date. I waited for the message. What I heard next chilled me from my head to my toes.

The caller only left a four-word message, "Watch your back, bitch!"

I couldn't tell if it was a woman or man because when the caller spoke, it sounds as if they were talking over a handkerchief. I replayed the message again, and then twice more after that. I didn't recognize the voice and went on to save the message to forward to my cell phone later when I arrived home.

With the events that occurred during the week, things were really starting to get way too creepy for me. I left the detective's card assigned to my case at home. I made a mental note to call him the first chance I got. I couldn't help but wonder who had it out for me especially since I was a very private person and kept to myself. I had no enemies to think of, so I couldn't figure out why someone would want to do harm to me. I was glad that I took Fred's advice and put my returned handgun in my purse.

"Better to be safe than sorry!" I said as I checked to make sure that the gun was still in my purse.

Chapter Fifteen
Compozer's Arrival

I was just about to leave the nail salon when my phone signaled that I had an email message. I logged into my email and saw that it was from Myles. Instantly, my face brightened up as I opened his email.

It read, *"Hey beautiful how are you today? I'll be in town tomorrow to meet with several record producers and want to see you badly. Will you be available for a night on the town and to show me your wonderful city? I sure hope and pray that you will do so. Call me on my cell phone and inform me of your decision as soon as you can. I'm at the airport on a layover and will be available for about another half hour. Take care Ms. Lady and hope to hear from you soon."*

I started to get butterflies in my stomach and began to get a little nervous. I was so happy to get the chance to meet Myles in person. We had been talking over the phone several times a day the last couple of weeks. The more we talked, I could feel my emotions becoming stronger towards him. He called me during his lunch break and would say that he pulled up my picture in order to imagine me talking with him face-to-face.

He was a wonderful man and been nothing but the perfect gentleman to me. When we talked with one another over the phone, I closed my eyes and listened to how his smooth and rich baritone voice flowed. It didn't hurt that the man was fine and had a sexy, sly grin.

He sent me an email containing several pictures of him that were taken for his new album cover. I noticed that he had striking brown eyes that could tame the wildest mare. His beard was trimmed to perfection and I bet he smelled good, too.

While Maria, my nail technician, was putting the finishing touches on my freshly-manicured toes, I took out my phone to call him. Myles answered after the second ring.

"Hello Ms. Lady," he answered. "How are you this afternoon?"

"I'm doing great and really happy to hear that you will be in town tomorrow," I said. "What time does your plane arrive?"

"I get in at 12:15, and will take the shuttle bus to the rental car place that is not too far from the airport. I have a room reserved and, once I get unpacked and settled, I will give you a call so that we can meet for dinner and, perhaps, a movie, if you like."

Now, at that point, I was thinking that he could stay in one of my spare bedrooms. So, before I knew it, I blurted out that he could stay with me if he'd like. For a brief second there was silence followed by a sexy chuckle.

Myles then said, "I would love nothing more than to be able to be near you in your beautiful home, but I don't want you to feel pressured. I'm not in the business of taking advantage of women."

"There's no problem, Myles. You're more that welcome to stay with me. I have three bedrooms with plenty of room to spare so come and stay—be my guest," I said.

"Are you sure that you'll be okay with that? I don't want to intrude and cause any problems, Brooke," he said.

"Do you have a pen and paper handy?"

"Hold on a second. I'll grab one out of my brief case," he said. I could hear him shuffling through his briefcase. "I'm ready, shoot!"

"I'm giving you directions to my house the quickest way that I know. I'm not that great on giving directions, but I won't get you lost," I told him confidently.

I delivered the address and directions. He repeated the directions back to confirm that he wrote them down correctly.

We continued our conversation for several minutes until the boarding announcement was made. He was in the first batch of boarders. I knew our conversation was about to end.

"That's me," he said. "I'm number fourteen so I guess I should get in line. I hate to let you go. I can talk with you forever."

"Don't miss the chance to get a good seat! We will have plenty of time to talk soon enough."

"Okay, Brooke, I shall see your beautiful face and pretty smile real soon."

"Have a safe flight and call me when your plane lands."

"Will do. I'll talk with you later."

"Bye," I softly whispered.

My mind was going a thousand miles a minute. I was making so many mental notes that my forehead should've looked like a post-it board.

"I need to go to the grocery store and get home to start preparing for dinner tomorrow night," I spoke aloud while frantically looking for a pen to create a grocery list to back up my thoughts.

I picked up my cell phone to speed dial Gabby's cell phone. After several rings, her voicemail picked up.

"Hello, you have reached the voice mail of Gabrielle. Unfortunately, I am unavailable to answer your call at the present moment. So, at the sound of the tone, please leave your name, telephone number and a brief, detailed message and I will return your call at my earliest availability."

'Gabby is never available present moment or the past. She is always on the go and seems to never be at home.'

I left her a brief, but detailed message to inform her that Myles would be coming into town the next day and that I, myself, might not be available. I urged her to call me soon.

As Maria was finishing up my toes, I reached into my billfold for a ten-dollar bill to leave her a tip. She always did a great job and my feet felt as smooth as a baby's bottom. I told her that I would see her in two weeks for a manicure and polish change. No one wanted to see three-inch husk with rust on a sista's foot!

As I was starting my truck, my cell phone rang. I looked at the caller ID and saw that it was Dante' calling. I sent him to voicemail. I hadn't spoken with him for several weeks. The night that the intruder tried to gain entry into my home, he did not return my call.

I knew with him being a businessman that he would check his messages on a regular basis and assumed that he heard the fear in my voice when I left him a message. So I wondered why, after all that time, did he even bother to call me.

The nerve! I know his ass got that message!'

My phone signaled that there was a new message. I ignored it and put my phone on the charger.

I was thinking to myself that I didn't have time for players or the likes of Dante'. I was disappointed because I thought that maybe we could have had something serious down the line. I felt that he was too much of a ladies' man and, despite my better judgment, gave him a chance anyway. Maybe he would get the hint and move on because, at that point, I would hate to have to hurt his feelings. It was true that Dante' was a desirable man and he was very much my cup of tea but being with a player was not for me.

"Next stop; Millshire Lane," I said. "I gotta get to the grocery store for items that will have this man falling in love with a sista in between bites!"

I couldn't wait to see Myles! I wondered what he would think about me when we both finally met in person for the first time.

'Looks like I'm making good time,' I thought as Will Downing and his leading lady, Brooke, hummed away on I-70.

Chapter Sixteen
The Way Love Goes

My alarm was crying out a hell-awful siren.

That was my signal to get my ass on up and get ready for that man. I spent the majority of the previous evening cleaning and straightening things around in the spare bedroom that Myles would be sleeping in.

"Don't no man like a dirty, nasty house," I said reminiscing about the days Mama had me cleaning for, what seemed like, days. "If she deals with it then she is dirty and nasty, too!"

"Keep a clean home and food on the stove and the man always comes home!" I could hear that as if it were yesterday.

After putting on fresh sheets and vacuuming the floor, I was pleased with the bedroom, which was a deep chocolate and tan color. I accented the room with deep red and burgundy throw pillows. I also placed fresh flowers on the nightstand that complimented the colors of the room.

I spent the better part of an hour trying to figure out what I was going to wear. I finally chose a black pair of form-fitting slacks, and a red off-the-shoulder blouse. After finding the right pair of black sling-back shoes, I began my search for the perfect pair of unmentionables. I never had been a thong type of woman unless I was wearing something that was fitted and would show a panty line. I picked out a pair of black and white laced bra and panty set that was revealing and sexy. After glancing at the clock on my nightstand, I saw that I had a little over an hour to get dressed before Myles arrived. I pinned my hair up, got into the shower and let the warm water drown me. I tried to let the soothing water emitting from the showerhead ease my nervous mind.

Myles had only seen pictures of me from my web page and a few that I sent him via email. In my mind I kept wondering would he be attracted to me because— let's be real— I was a full-figured woman.

He said in recent conversations, that size didn't matter to him and that he loved his woman to be on the thick side. The look of skin with bones jutting out from the rib cage was very unflattering. I was a "fluffy" girl so I knew that I had to always put my best foot forward just to dispel the myths about larger people.

I got out of the shower, quickly dried off and reached for my cucumber melon lotion and after-shower body spray. I had packed on a facial mask before I had gotten into the shower and then rinsed it off once I had pampered my skin with my favorite perfume. As I was tidying the bathroom, I heard the telephone ringing in my bedroom. I managed to answer on the third ring before my voicemail kicked on.

"Hey, Ms. Lady," Myles said.

"Hi handsome. Have you arrived, yet?"

"As a matter of fact, I have. My plane landed about thirty minutes ago and now I'm waiting for the rental car agent to bring my rental car around front."

"Wow, so you'll be on your way to my house soon. Do you still have the directions to get here?"

"Yes I do," he said. "I've read over them so much that I've practically memorized them."

I could hear the rental agent in the background telling Myles that his car was ready and that she wanted to review a few quick details with him about the policy.

"Brooke, I have a few minor details to go over before I leave here. I will call you back when I'm near your home."

"Go ahead and do your thing. I look forward to seeing you. I'm so nervous and this will give me some time to calm my nerves before your arrival," I said.

I heard him chuckle that sexy laugh of his and I knew that everything was going to be fine.

"You have no reason to be nervous," he said. "I'm just as excited to see you as you are me and, I promise, I won't bite."

We both hung up and then I resumed prepping myself for our evening. After getting dressed, I sat at my vanity table to apply a light coat of foundation, eye shadow, and a coat of tinted lip-gloss.

"I need to buy stock in MAC make-up! This is probably about three-thousand dollars' worth of great make-up. I'll die without my MAC!" I laughed as I took in a colorful view of make-up spreading from one end of the table to the other.

I unpinned and combed out my mid-shoulder length hair. The steam from the shower had set my hair perfectly and all I had to do was tussle with a few strands here and there. Finally, to top it off, I applied a little oil sheen and hairspray.

I take a long look in my full-length mirror to make sure that everything was in its place and that the twins were where they were supposed to be.

After making sure that everything was straight in my bedroom, it was time to set an enticing ambiance. The atmosphere was the most important part of any date. Lighting and aromas must be on point.

Flipping through my CDs I found myself having a hard time trying to decide the right music with Myles being a musician and all. I was trying to find his next-to-favorite artist.

"Okay, I'll put this three-series mixed CD in and let them all play. This way, he'll get more than what he wants— musically speaking!" I said aloud.

I then lit a few floral-fragranced incense sticks and placed them around the house.

I was so nervous that, after several minutes of sitting on my couch, I began to pace back and forth throughout the house. I wanted to make sure that everything was perfect and in its place before Myles arrived.

"Brooke calm down girl! Inhale-exhale-inhale-exhale," I said, inhaling the garden-like scents and exhaling my nervousness."

I grabbed a book of poetry called the "Oral Elixir" that I had purchased several months ago. The title, as well as the picture on the book, drove me insane because I had no idea what the title meant. I had a big, nasty assumption about what it meant. Time, work and all this drama caused me to shelf that baby until I was ready to find out for certain. I took a seat in the over-stuffed chair placed by my living room window. It rained the previous night so the streets were still damp from the morning dew. The natural light shone in from outside and gave my living room a peaceful glow.

I was mesmerized as I looked around my lovely piece of home as if seeing it for the very first time. Everything seemed different for me even though I knew every inch of my home. The peaceful ambience had calmed my restless nerves. I was finally able to concentrate solely on Myles and nothing else. I'd read a couple of the poems and had to put the book down.

'Oh, good Lord, did I turn the heat on? The book is fire.'
I needed to read it on my own alone "girl time."

Myles called and informed me that he was close. Shortly thereafter, a black SUV pulled into my driveway. Several seconds later, Myles emerged from the truck.

What I saw next made me gasp, hold my breath, and say, "Oh my goodness."

Chapter Seventeen
His Entrance

Words could not adequately express what I saw outside my window. Myles stood about six-foot tall, broad shouldered, well-trimmed beard and sporting a shiny bald head. He looked my way, smiled and showed how deep his dimples were. He was a well-put together brother and I was surprised that some woman hadn't snatched him up by now. I was sure many had tried but obviously failed. If they had won him over, then he wouldn't have been at my place now.

He pressed the trunk release button of the SUV and grabbed two bags before closing the trunk. Afterwards, he engaged the alarm on his ride and headed towards my front porch.

I took a deep breath, counted to five and headed to my front door. He rang my doorbell just as I opened the door and I could see that he was beaming all over.

"Hey you, I'm so glad that you made it safely," I said as I opened the door wide for him.

"Hello Ms. Lady," he said stepping in. "You are absolutely beautiful and stunning."

"Thank you! You are very handsome and sharp looking if I might say so myself," I said.

I closed the door behind him while he set his bags on the floor by the couch, which gave me a chance to check him out again. Suddenly, he walked toward my direction. I couldn't help but to smile at this confident man, who was walking toward me.

He grabbed both of my hands and kissed both of them ever so gently and wrapped his arm around my waist to pull me closer to him.

"I am so glad you are finally here, Myles," I said.

He smiled a sexy sly grin, then gave me the most wonderful hug that I'd ever had in my life. It felt so good that no kiss was needed to accompany the hug. I didn't want to let him go. I felt safe and secure. I was dizzy from his intoxicating cologne and mesmerized by his warm gentle embrace.

After several minutes, we stepped away from each other and I begin to blush from the way that he was looking at me. It felt as if he was taking all of me to the inside of his heart.

"Grab your bags and let me show you to your room, and then I'll give you a tour of my home," I said.

"Sure thing, Brooke. I love how you have laid out your living room and the color scheme is similar to my own taste," he said.

I could see that he was admiring several of my jazz paintings that I had strategically hung on the wall of the room that he would be sleeping in.

"Who's the artist of these pieces of work, Brooke?"

"Blair Adagio is the artist who painted the jazz pieces," I answered. "She is from Ghana and has been on the scene for a very short time. She has a waiting list for six months for some of her pieces because of the high demand for her work."

"I can see why," he said. "She's very good and I would love to purchase a piece or two to place in my studio."

"I can give you the address to her website. Then you can view her entire collection. There are also several links of several other artists that you may like later."

"Thank you. I look forward to browsing through her site. From the looks of it, I know she has a great selection," he said while still appearing to be mesmerized by the artwork.

I found myself staring and admiring his package while he studied my art. I liked the way that he tilted his head to the side and then rested his pointer finger at the corner of his mouth. I guessed that was the reason why I didn't hear him call my name.

"Brooke, are you okay?"

I snapped back from the world of naughty and laughed out loud.

"I'm fine, just watching you admiring the paintings. Can I get you something to eat and drink? I know that you're hungry after such a long flight."

"As a matter of fact, I am both," he said. "As you can see, I don't pass up too many meals when I have the time to enjoy eating," he said while patting his solid belly, which made a very funny sound.

"My hectic schedule has kept me extremely busy, and usually it's grab a bite here and there when I can."

"Well, follow me to the kitchen and I'll fix you a plate with a tall, ice-cold glass of strawberry lemonade."

"Watch yourself now, Ms. Lady," he said. "I told you that I don't pass up a good meal, especially prepared by such a beautiful woman."

At that comment, I begin to blush uncontrollably and had to look away for a brief minute.

Myles asked where the bathroom was in order to freshen up before eating. I grabbed his hand and led him in the direction of the bathroom at the same time that Donte popped in my mind.

"Now cha'mon back when ya done now. Don't have me waiting all day to throw down," I joked putting on a fake accent.

"Girl you are so crazy! I'll be there," Myles said while his laughter followed him into the bathroom.

When I lifted the lid from the skillet, tantalizing aromas filled the air in the kitchen. The smell of roasted garlic and basil simmered in my skillet.

"Tonight's entire meal is Chicken Marsala with Fettuccini Alfredo, tossed salad with romaine lettuce, and garlic bread," I announced in a playful manner when he came back into the room.

"That does sound good, Ms. Lady," Myles said softly. I was totally unaware he was standing in the kitchen.

"Dang, this kitchen is top of the line, Grade A, clean, neat, and smelling good! I'm gonna eat here all the time!" Myles said while leaning against the counter. "Can I help? I'm ready to chow because I can't let you hear my stomach roar again!

"Something sure smells good. You have a brother's mouthwatering. I can't wait to eat. You know how it is with airplane meals. They give you a packet of peanuts and a half a can of soda. It's a shame that the airlines can charge you an arm and a leg, but can only give you prison-type rations that they consider as a meal. So forgive me if I bring a huge appetite to the table," he rambled.

"Well, come on and make yourself comfortable and have a seat," I said, eagerly. "I just have to fill our plates and then it's time to eat."

After placing the plates and lemonade on the table, Myles rushed to my side to pull out my seat.

"Now you may sit."

I placed my napkin in my lap and then asked Myles if he would say grace to bless this wonderful meal. He took my hand and bowed his head in prayer as I did the same.

"Dear Lord, we come to you and ask that you bless this meal prepared for us. We thank you for your many blessings and ask that you continue to keep us safe and in your grace. These and all other blessings we ask, Amen," he humbly prayed.

I then looked at him and thanked him for such an eloquent prayer. We both grabbed our forks and began to chow down on the meal before us.

"Umm, umm, umm!" Myles said after taking a bite. "Not only did you put your foot in this, but your ankle, knee and elbow. This is absolutely wonderful and, never in my life, have I tasted something that seems to *melt* in my mouth and play with my taste buds."

I wondered if he would enjoy the meal since it was the first time I prepared this particular dish. I wanted to do something different. No Big Momma meals. I was tired of eating like that. I was pleased that it tasted good and, from the looks of it, Myles had no complaints, either.

We talked while we ate and it seemed like we were catching up on lost time. I was looking at the man who sat before me and thought, *'What wonderful eyes he has.'*

His expressions showed and his eyes sparkled when he laughed. He also has the most amazing dimples that I'd ever seen. His beard and goatee were meticulously groomed down to the nines. He was truly a sexy, big and tall brother whom I most definitely didn't mind getting to know much, much better.

It was getting hot in the room and I grabbed a napkin to wipe my brow and fan myself gently.

'Did I turn the heat on?'

We continued to talk about the recent events of our lives— including my home invasion. Myles asked if there were any new details as to who tried to break into my home. I told him that the detective on my case was on vacation for the week, but promised to get back with me as soon as he got back into town. I told Myles that I had received a threatening phone call at my job and had forwarded the message to the detective, also.

Myles showed a look of concern on his face and then said, "Be careful, Brooke, and be aware of your surroundings at all times until they can catch who did this to you. I know that you have a good head on your shoulders and that you can take care of yourself well, but I want you to be safe and sound no matter what the cost may be.

"When you told me what happened, I was worried and concerned for you. At that point, I really couldn't wait to see you. You've touched something deep from within that I had put away to protect—my heart and my emotions, that is. I think that you're a truly beautiful and smart woman, Brooke. If allowed, I want to get to know you more than just on that friendship level. Who knows what the future may hold but, hopefully, I will be a part of yours and you a part of mine."

He took my hand and kissed it, all the while never taking his eyes from mine.

I wondered what color my cheeks were. I was blushing uncontrollably and he knew it because he let out one of his sexy chuckles that made my blood pressure raise a few numbers. To try to ease the obvious flirting that Myles was doing, I asked him if he left room for the strawberry cheesecake dessert that I had made the night before.

"Yes ma'am, but I must tell you that if all your dishes are as perfect as this one, you're going to make me lose my hour-glass figure," he joked with a hearty laugh. He said that he would clean the table while I put coffee on and grabbed the cheesecake from the refrigerator.

We talked well into the evening and, before we knew it, the sun was setting. I suggested that he grab some rest and maybe we could watch a DVD if he was up to it later on. He said that he wanted to shower then take a short nap and would take me up on my offer to watch a movie. I told him that there were clean towels in the bathroom located on the counter that I had set out for him and, if he needed anything, he was free to let me know.

"Thanks, Ms. Lady. I do appreciate all your hospitality and the good cooking. You better watch out; you'll have a permanent house guest if you're not careful."

'Funny thing is, I believe him.'

I followed him out of the kitchen and went into the living room to set the alarm for the night. As I headed toward my bedroom, I paused at Myles' door and watched him start to unpack his luggage. For a few seconds, I studied his stance and how confidently he moved. Watching closely, I admired how Myles placed his clothing in the draws that I had made room for. I then moved further into the room and asked him if he needed any help unpacking.

"Sure, I can always use the help. I tried to pack lightly, but still managed to probably over pack since I had to do so at the last minute," he said.

He handed me a clothes' bag that had a few of his suits and dress slacks and shirts. They were pressed and neatly hung on hangers from the dry cleaners, which had the cleaner's logo printed on the hanger sleeves. Myles had a distinctive style of dress that complimented his musical background.

'He smells soooooooooo good!' I thought.

As I turned around to ask him if he needed anything else, he was standing right behind me I bumped right into his chest. I gasped and then held my hand to my chest where my heart began to rapidly beat. He leaned closer to me, placed my hands on his chest while driving his lips to mine. He softly kissed me on my lips. The touch sent a sensation that rippled through my arms towards my neck. He then kissed the corners of my mouth and lingered on to the side of my neck. My world began to spin and I felt slightly light head.

Myles put his long arms around my waist and pulled me even closer into him. I could feel the heat from his body and the smell from his knee-weakening cologne was only making my insides stir even more.

'I luvs a good love smellin' man!'

We kissed and held each other for several seconds until we both finally pulled away from one another. I looked into his eyes and saw the desire that he had for me. I was sure my face reflected the same energy and passion. He then took my right hand and kissed the palm of it.

"You are truly a beautiful and amazing woman," Myles said. "Please forgive me if I came on too strong but, for some reason, you are undeniable. Even if nothing else was to happen, being in your presence, smelling your essence is heaven. It seems as if I was under your spell, Ms. Lady."

I was totally speechless, which was unusual for me since I was very vocal about my opinions and emotions at any given moment. I reached to stroke his beard and then began to trace the outline of his lips with the tips of my fingers.

"There was no harm done and I enjoyed the wonderful kiss," I said. "It allowed me to get even closer."

We were so close to one another that there was hardly room to move around. I hesitated and moved in closer until our lips were barely touching one another. We then started to kiss one another again, softly but passionately. Myles grabbed me around my waist and pulled me closer until I could feel that his furnace was back on. Our tongues intertwined with one another and our breathing became sporadic but, yet, in sync as we continued to kiss. I could feel him getting excited and he didn't try to hide the fact that he was fully aroused. He then glided his hand underneath my blouse and gently caressed my rigid nipples, which took my breath away at first touch.

'Long time since a sista felt like, hey now!' I moaned in excitement and pleasure as he continued to stimulate me.

He was so into making me feel his desire that it felt like the room was spinning. I had to lean against the wall to avoid collapsing onto the floor because I was so weak in the knees. He then unbuttoned my blouse and slipped my slacks off and put them both on the chair next to the bed. I had only my bra and panties left on, which were eventually discarded like the rest of my clothes.

I was a little self-conscious about being completely nude standing in front of Myles, but he set my mind at ease when he said, "You have a lovely body. You should never be ashamed or shy about how you look, Brooke. You are the perfect woman for me and I plan to show you how much you mean to me tonight."

He undressed and stood before me nude; never taking his eyes from mine. His figure was that of a football linebacker and he carried his weight well. I ran my finger against his smooth cocoa skin and tracked my fingers along his face and the outline of his beard.

'Yeah, I got a thang for men with that ever-so-sexy 'Gerald Levert' beard. He was the coldest man to wear a beard ever; rest his soul!'

We began to kiss again and the heat and fire within the both of us was so intense that the fire department could have been on its way, for all I knew. My breath was completely taken away. Then, in one swift motion, he lifted my body and carried me to the bed that was prepared for him. He slid the comforter back with one hand and laid me down on my back with the other. He slid under the comforter and laid next to me and I could feel the heat emitting from his skin, which made me more excited by the minute.

We resumed our kissing and he murmured how he was glad to have me in his arms and to himself. His tender touches made my entire body tingle from deep within. His lips slipped down from my mouth, my neck and then to my breasts. He kissed each of them individually as if they were a special prize that he won. I moaned in ecstasy as he teased my ridged nipples and then moved to kiss my stomach.

I knew what time it was when he spread my thighs apart and lovingly kissed the inside of both of them. I didn't know how he managed to find one of my many erogenous zones, but he did. I flexed my back as he began to separate my secret set of lips with his tongue. He took his sweet time and licked me like he was cleaning the plate from which he feasted off of at dinner. He confidently whispered in my ear, his eyes never leaving mine while he slipped a condom on.

I grabbed on to my sheets and held on for the ride of my life. The first time that I climaxed, I thought that I was losing my mind. I was totally out of control as I embraced and welcomed two more orgasms.

I screamed and held on to the back of his head for dear life.

I gradually floated down from my high, but that didn't stop Myles from pleasing me continuously. I had three orgasms and he finally stopped after I begged and pleaded.

His face glistened with the juices of my love zone and he wasn't in the least bit ready to end our love making. I could see that he was extremely hard and, soon after, he slid into me slowly but methodically.

"Myles you feel exotic to me," I said

"Exotic, baby?"

"Yeah, like some stuff I've never had before. Something so special you have to travel far away, and hunt for. When you find it—it's rare, it's all exotic," I explained gasping in between each thrust.

"I'm in heaven and don't want to leave," he said and began to thrust deeper and harder.

I squeezed my vagina and welcomed every inch of him greedily. I was experiencing pure ecstasy, none of which I had ever felt before. He looked at me in amazement as I squeezed him and clamped down on his handle bar. That only intensified the experience between the two of us and, before long, we both were going to come with one another.

"Oh yes!" he exclaimed and thrust himself even harder and faster.

"Come with me," I said and wrapped my legs around his back very tightly.

The next moment, I had a sensation of thick white lightening escaping my vagina as I pulled Myles closer to me.

'Damn, the condom came off!!!!'

When he moaned loudly I knew that he was climaxing and it was because of me. His warm juices flowed intensely and freely inside me. I came a split second after he did and moaned out his name over and over again. Myles buckled and rolled over on his back.

I then laid on his chest and said nothing as we both were still in the midst of this orgasmic heaven. He caressed my back and smoothed the hair from my face. I was completely speechless and fulfilled at the same moment.

Myles spoke the words that I wasn't expecting him to say.

"I'm loving hard on you, Brooke. I have always had it for you from the first time I first laid eyes on you."

There was no doubt in my mind that he meant every word because I, too, realized that I was falling for him. It doesn't take forever and a million fights and make-up sessions to figure out real love.

I looked him directly in the eyes and spoke the same words he relayed to me.

"I'm loving hard on you too, Myles. I never want this moment to end and want you in my life," I firmly stated as I leaned deeply into his chest.

"If I can help it, I won't have it any other way. I have so many plans running through my head for us and our future together and, one day, I want you for my wife."

He then reached over into his carry-on bag beside the bed and pulled out a small jewelry box and opened it.

'Oh hells naw! Is he about to do what I think? It's only been three months since we have been talking and knowing Momma always said, 'You know the real deal, baby, when it approaches you.'

"Brooke, will you do the honor of becoming my wife and marry me?"

I was utterly taken aback by his request to become his wife. Tears began to flow freely. I said the first thing that came to my mind, "Yes I will marry you. I'd love nothing better."

We embraced each other and I really began to cry. I cried happy tears because I knew Myles was the man meant for me. It was as if I was looking to find my soul mate and he found me in just the right time.

He took the ring from the box and I saw how gorgeous the ring truly was. It was a twenty-four carat, white gold, solitaire princess cut, diamond ring. It also had a matching wedding band with other stones cascading around it that sparkled with the hues of a rainbow. I was so excited, I couldn't wait for him to place the ring on my finger. I kissed and hugged him tightly and told him that I was the luckiest woman alive.

I couldn't wait to call my mom and Gabby to tell them the exciting news. Over the past couple of months, I had told my mom a lot about Myles and she was anxious to meet the young man who captured her baby girl's heart and attention. Since Myles had a meeting with the record executives for most of the morning the next day, we decided to take my mom and step-dad out to dinner and give them the news. I reached over Myles to grab the cordless. I had to call Gabby. After several rings, her voicemail kicked in and, once again, she was unavailable to take my call.

A few days before, I had text messaged her and she responded saying that she was out of the country for a few days on a photo shoot with a famous clothing designer and would not be back home for a week or more. Gabby didn't let grass grow under her feet for long and was always on the go. I made a mental note to text her and inform her of recent events.

Myles and I made love again and cuddled throughout the night until we both drifted off to sleep in each other's arms. I prayed that, if this was all a dream, I would not ever desire to wake up. I wanted to embed that exact moment in my mind forever.

Myles was such a wonderful man and I promised to make it my life's mission making him— wait, the Lord first then him —happy! I knew this was exactly where I belonged and, for the night, I didn't plan on going anywhere.

It was hard seeing Myles leave after spending many blissful days with him. We enjoyed each other's company and never wanted it to end. In between his meetings, we spoke of our future plans with each other and set our wedding date for June twenty-eighth the following summer.

My mom and step-dad were ecstatic about our wonderful news of marriage. Fred and Myles hit it off like they were old friends and mom was happy that she would have such a pleasant and handsome son-in-law. He was able to meet my sister, her daughter and grandmother when we attended church services, and I could have sworn my grandmother was flirting with my man. I couldn't help but to laugh. At eighty-nine, my grandmother still had it going on and did not miss a step.

We dropped off his rental car near the airport the day before he left, so that I would be able to see him off the next day. It was extremely hard seeing him leave and I knew that I was going to cry. We talked non-stop until it was announced that his flight was about to board. He stood and took my hands and pulled me up to hug me. I had to look up since he was several feet taller than I, and I gazed lovingly into his beautiful brown eyes. He wiped the tears from my eyes and kissed me as if we were alone.

"You know that this isn't goodbye and I will see you at the end of the month. I have a few loose ends to take care of like putting my house on the market before I move here permanently. I will try to get back to you as soon as possible. Since the company I work for agreed to let me work from home, I can set up shop anywhere I please."

As a graphic designer for a prestigious Fortune 500 company, Myles was able to produce magnificent creations that warranted his six-figure salary. Plus, his music career was sealed with a recording contract and his album would be released later that fall.

We walked over to his gate kissed and hugged once more. Since 9/11 regulations prohibited me from entering the passenger area, I stood at the glass partition to watch him leave.

"I love you, baby, and I will call you as soon as I land," he assured me. "You be careful on the ride home and think only pleasant thoughts. Know that this is not permanent and only temporary and I will see you soon."

"I love you too, with all my heart. Thank you for the wonderful time that we were able to spend with one another. I'll miss you something terrible but knowing that you'll be here forever with me, keeps me happy."

We embraced one last time and he walked away to board his plane. He looked back, waved, smiled until his image faded out of sight. I didn't want to leave until his plane was in the blue skies.

No sooner than I made it to my car, I began to cry again. Myles had touched my heart and soul and left his mark embedded there. I was to become his bride next year and it was a wonderful moment to envision as I leaned on my car looking up at the promising blue skies. I was finally happy with a man who was meant for me and he made it clear that he wasn't going anywhere.

As I pulled away from the airport, I looked at the sky and saw many planes flying to unknown destinations. I couldn't help but wonder if Myles was in one of them looking for me. I took the long route home while enjoying the sunshine and wanted to reflect on my time spent with Myles. If it was all a dream, I never wanted to wake up.

Chapter Eighteen
The Invite

It seemed as if my job was never done. I had to bring some paperwork home over the weekend in order to complete my report that was due on Monday. I had a presentation to deliver to the board members at the law firm. I wanted to show that, if we commercialized the firm and raised the attention of the public's eye, it would draw even more clients to us. Having the low-end service fees for the low-income and having the best innocent and acquittal rates was where we created home runs.

As I was reading over the rough draft of my proposal, there was a knock at my front door. I bookmarked the page that I was reading and headed to my door. I looked through the peephole to see that it was the regular postman in my neighborhood and that he had a package and several letters in his hand to give to me. When I opened the door, he greeted me with a smile and handed me my mail.

"Have a good day ma'am," he said.

I thanked him and bid him the same.

Before I left work on Friday, I asked Shelia to overnight me the completed paperwork of the summer interns so that I could assign each one their positions come Monday. Both of the interns were eager and could not wait until they were settled in their own office. The big man was looking for fresh, raw, and hungry-at-heart attorneys. They couldn't have a soft heart if they were going to be prosecutors and they couldn't be dumb trying to defend someone, either. I had high expectations for each of them and knew that both of them will excel and make great progress at the firm.

'I love seeing sistas climb that ladder!'

I placed my overnight package on my desk next to the proposal that I was working on and began to sort through my mail. Several letters were from the local utility companies that I stacked on top of one another to look at when I paid my monthly bills. There were also a few fliers announcing various two-day sales and coupons taking thirty-five percent off my purchase that are attached to it. I quickly tossed those in the trash and thought that I didn't need to go anywhere near a mall for the next several months.

For the last two months, I'd been splurging on myself— all induced by the stressful recent events. I felt there was a need to cut my spending by more than half. I took all of my credit cards —except for one— and mailed them to my mother to keep for three months. I told her not to bend and give them back to me no matter how much I cried, begged or had a childish fit in the middle of the living room floor. She said that she was going to hold me to it no matter what and — deep down inside — I knew that she would.

As I got to the bottom of the stack of mail and fliers, I noticed a postcard invitation addressed to me. It was facing backside up so I began to read the invitation that was announcing an upcoming *Swinger's Ball* to be held at the Crystal Ball club the following weekend. I read the invitation twice before turning over to view the front cover. I couldn't think of who would send me an invite to such an event. The thought of attending a venue like that would never cross my mind. I flipped the front over and saw a crowd of men and women gracing the front cover all posing for the camera. What I saw next made me gasp. I was sure my eyes bulged out a few inches.

Standing between two scantily-dressed buxom women, was none other than Dante'. He was dressed in a black silk tank and white slacks while two women on each side of him had on matching bra tops and barely-there bikinis. After I picked my bottom lip up from the floor, I flipped the invitation over again to see who had sent me the invite. There was no name on the printed card, just the date time and location of the event. For the life of me I couldn't figure out who thought they knew me well enough to send me an invite to a *swinger's ball*.

I needed to get down to the bottom of it because too many weird and crazy events had happened to me for what seemed like no reason at all. I couldn't figure out for the life of me, whose toes I stepped on to deserve to be stalked, harassed, as well as having my personal space invaded. If it was the last thing that I did, I would find out the culprit behind all the nonsense once and for all.

I reached over for my cell phone atop my desk to search for Dante's phone number. I had it stored in my phone book. After finding his direct office number, I punched in the seven digits on my home cordless phone.

After several rings he picked up the phone and said, "Hello Ms. Brooke. It's good that you finally called me back. I left you several messages and emails and was wondering if you had given me the boot and kicked me to the curb."

"Hello Dante'," I said dryly, ignoring his bullshit intro getting right to business.

"I called you to ask you about something that I received in the mail this afternoon. I received an invitation to an upcoming swinger's ball to be held next Saturday. To my complete surprise, there was a picture of you on the front of the invite. Were you the person who sent this to me?"

There was a brief moment of silence and then he told me that he was on his way to my home and abruptly disconnected the phone conversation.

I held the phone away from my ear to see if he actually hung up on me because I didn't expect that type of response from him. I was thinking that the conversation went well.

'Yeah right. I know that I have to prepare myself for what may happen next with Dante'. I am expecting the unexpected! A hurt and rejected brother is bad news. Dante' has and intimidating attitude towards many people and he usually comes off as a 'no nonsense' type of man. I'm wondering how he's going to explain why he is smiling like a cat that ate the bird with two women who obviously aren't two nuns from the Vatican wearing next to nothing.'

I was eager to hear his explanation and to learn how many excuses he had for sending me and invitation that wasn't my cup of tea.

I then quickly headed toward my bedroom to freshen up my face and run a comb through my hair. I was dressed comfortably in white girly shorts and a pink tee that said, "Kiss me" with red heart-shaped lips since it was the weekend. I applied a quick coat of light pink lip gloss and gathered my courage in order to deal with what was to come next with Dante'.

While I was waiting for Dante' to arrive, I opened the envelope that contained the files that I asked Shelia to send to me. I had the two-summer interns type what they thought their strengths and weakness were when it came to certain areas such as customer service, typing, sending facsimiles and public speaking —all of which was expected at times if we fail to keep legal aid staffers at all times.

Several minutes into reading about my two interns, I heard a car engine as Dante's SUV pulled into my driveway. I instantly began to have butterflies in my stomach and took several deeps breaths to calm myself and to get my thoughts back on track. I figured he'd get my "North Pole" shoulder. As Dante' emerged from his truck, I could see that he was visibly shaken and upset about the situation. At that point, I really didn't know what to think but, in order to get down to the bottom of things, I needed answers. I shut my computer off and met Dante' at the door before he could knock.

"Hello Dante'," I said as I opened the front door, "Come in and have a seat."

I asked him if he wanted something to drink. He declined. I sat down in the chair opposite of the couch where he was sitting in order to get a full view of him while we discussed the situation. I pointed to the invitation that was sitting on my coffee table, front-side up, so that he could see himself on the front of the invitation. He stared at it blankly.

My first question to him was whether or not he sent me the invitation to the swinger's ball.

"No and I don't know who would send you an invite," he said defensively. "I can say that I have attended several of the swinger's balls in order to promote some of my rap groups, but that is strictly that. If I want to continue to live the lifestyle that I do, I have to promote and make a living somehow.

"Many of my clients make appearances around several clubs throughout the city and, as the head of my company, I introduce many of my new up-and-coming acts hoping they can perform at these joints. There is nothing more. I enjoy what I do and I do it the best. Many people out there want to jeopardize my company and what I've built; but I'm not having that. I will be there this weekend to introduce one of my rap groups that recently signed with my record label.

"Maybe you should attend so we both can find out who sent you the invitation."

I give him a run-down of all the mayhem that had been going on in my life. Finally I admitted that his invitation sounded like a great idea.

I didn't divulge too much information because, at that point, I didn't know who was targeting me. From the look on his face, he seemed to be in total disbelief. He asked if I needed his help with finding the culprit and have them charged for the vandalism to my home and property. He went on to say that he had a team of private detectives at his beck and call. I figured, with the industry that he was in, he needed to have many of his clients' reputations thoroughly checked. Tempting as it sounded, I told him that it would not be necessary.

"Whatever you say, baby girl," he said. "If you need me, there's nothing that you can't ask for. I'm sorry that I was unreachable that night that the intruder tried to break into your home. I was out entertaining several of my clients. When entertaining, I turn the ringer off on my phone.

"It was not till several days that I checked my messages and heard your message. I'm so sorry that I wasn't able to be there for you and want you to know that you can depend on me for anything," he said.

'Yeah right; this nut must think that I believe his game.'

So I let him ramble on for a few more seconds while I contemplated my next move. I've had to be street savvy a time or two in my thirty-two years of living on this earth, but I must say Dante' would be my greatest challenge.

After several seconds of his rambling, he stopped and asked if I was okay. I let him know that everything was good and that I would be ready Saturday at seven so he could pick me up for the Swinger's Ball. He had a confused look on his face as if he was puzzled about my reaction to his comments. I chuckled and then let him know that I was good.

"I just want to get down to the bottom of this and move on with my life," I said. "Someone out there is targeting me for no particular reason and I cannot allow anyone to do harm to me— if I can help it. I thank you for your offer to help me and I truly appreciate it Dante'."

"Believe it or not, I do have strong feelings for you, Brooke, and would like to continue to pursue something more with you. I've never met a woman like you and I think that we both can make something special if you allow me to be a part of your life," he sadly pleaded.

At that point, I let him know that certain things had changed concerning him and I. I told him, once all the drama has settled down in my life, that I would sit down and talk with him and let him know where we both stood.

I could tell that my response didn't sit very well with him but he wasn't going to push the issue. I stood to head for the front door to see him out when he grabbed me by my waist and pulled me closer to him. He looked deep into my eyes as if searching for answers and then leaned over to kiss my forehead. Once again, I inhaled his deep, rich scent from his cologne and placed my hand on his chest to stop him from doing anything more. He nodded as if knowing that he should not push the issue and kissed my hand.

"I'll call you in the middle of the week to make sure that you're going."

"Sounds like a plan to me. I shall see you soon, Dante', and thank you for coming by."

"Take care, baby girl, and call me if you need me— no matter the time of day. Please be careful and be watchful. I don't know what fool is out there but, if I ever get a hand on them, it won't be nice," he said.

I assured him that I would call him if something should arise. He bid me farewell with the tilt of his head and then got into his car. I watched him back out of the driveway and head towards Elmwood then finally disappear out of my sight.

As I closed the door, a million things were running through my head and I felt slightly flushed. I had to calm my nerves and get a hold of myself if I wanted to function to my full capacity. I knew that I had to finish my proposal and continue to read over the interns' files. I turned my computer back on and settled myself in for a long weekend ahead. No sooner than I get started my cell phone rings. I looked at the caller I.D. It was Jonathan, my ex-husband, calling from his home phone.

I really didn't feel like dealing with that headache so I pushed the "End" button on my cell phone and let it go the voicemail. If he left a message, I wouldn't check it till later. I hadn't heard from him since I introduced that *Babe Ruth* side of me when I did a disabling act by beating his knee caps off. My mind was a million miles away from the work that I had ahead of me and I had to force myself to concentrate and get that out of the way before Monday— couldn't look dumb and unprepared at my own presentation.

I flipped the Swinger's Ball invitation over again and couldn't help but look at Dante' as he grinned for the camera. I wondered if the answers that I had were contained within the invite and hoped for a resolution to all the drama. It had to come to an end soon.

Chapter Nineteen
The Swinger's Ball

Dante' arrived at my home shortly after six-thirty. He was dressed in a white shirt with matching pants and shoes. His beard and head were freshly shaven and he had on strikingly debonair attire. That night, I wore a strapless black dress that came just above my knees with wrap-around four-inch open-toed heels. My hair was pinned up with a silver rhinestone comb and ringlets framed my face. Dante' picked me up in a sporty drop-top black BMW ZR Roadster II.

I asked him how many cars he owned.

"I have three including this one which was given to me as a gift from one of my clients once his album went platinum."

"Must be nice," I said. "I wish I were so lucky to have a client give me a free car."

"It's not that easy. Trust me. There's a price for everything. I pulled a lot of strings for this particular client and his album blew up overnight. When his album sales took off, we both benefited from it and, to return the favor, he had the car delivered to me as a surprise at his album debut party held a few months back," he explained.

I still considered him lucky to have a car given to him no matter what the circumstance might have been.

The car had all the amenities that you could ask for and then some. It had a remote control attached to the key ring that could raise and lower the convertible top and, in the dashboard, was a DVD/computer touchscreen that could control the radio, seats and climate in the car. Dante' went on to explain that it had several sensors throughout the vehicle that could adapt to his own personal settings. Everything about this car screamed high-tech and lots of cash. I hated to see his insurance bill each month and I was sure his deductible was through the roof.

He raised the top so the wind won't blow my hair out of place.

"You look nice this evening, Brooke, and the dress really becomes you."

"Thank you," I blushed. "You look handsome, yourself, and white is very flattering on you."

After several minutes of silence, we both spoke at the same time. He asked if I was nervous and I asked was he ready for the night ahead.

"You first," he said.

"I am more anxious than nervous and, hopefully, I find the answers that I'm looking for.

"You're next; are you ready for tonight's events?"

"Well, since I'm announcing my recent group, I'm used to it. These groups of rappers are out of Philly and they are a crowd stopper. Some of their lyrics are raw and off the chain, but they know how to keep the crowd going. I'm prepared and ready for whatever happens, baby girl. I will protect not only myself but also you— at all costs."

'Well where was this Negro when someone was trying to knock the hinges of my damn backdoor?'

"Trust me when I say that you're in good hands tonight."

I wished I felt as assured as he did as we pulled in front of the Crystal Ball Club. As Dante' stepped from the car, a valet opened the passenger side door for me. I grabbed my purse and extended my hand to Dante' and stepped from the vehicle. I could hear the music pumping out the foundation of the club, before we entered. There were several bouncers at the front door checking the men and women before they entered the club. As we approached, one of the muscle-bound goons who recognized Dante' pulled back the velvet rope in order for us to pass through. Dante' shook his hand and extended the usual greeting that most brothers use when they know and acknowledge one another.

Once inside, I could see that the club was almost full to capacity. There were scantily-clothed women with barely-there skirts and tops. Compared to some of the women, I felt overdressed. Most men were dressed in slacks and shirts since the dress code of no jeans and tennis shoes was firmly enforced. Dante' led me to the VIP section of the club that was centered toward the middle in front of the stage. He pulled out my seat and then sat directly beside me on the right.

I felt totally uncomfortable and out of place while Dante' looked as if he fit in and was in his own element. I sat as close to Dante' as possible so that no one could mistake me as being alone. Several minutes later, a server came over to take our drink orders and placed tantalizing appetizers in the center of table. I ordered a glass of white wine and Dante' ordered a premium beer along with a bottle of Rosé Moet. The DJ was spinning a hip-hop rap mix on the turntable while dancers, clothed in red and black costumes, danced in a cage hanging from the ceiling. There were several couples on the dance floor grinding and swaying to the music. I could see quite a few rooms located throughout the perimeter of the club that had no doors but drapes to conceal their occupants. I could only imagine what happened behind those closed drapes with the occasion being a swinger's ball and all.

I was so drawn to the activities in the club that I didn't hear Dante' calling my name until he touched me on the shoulder. He told me that my wine was sitting in front of me and then asked if I was all right. I reassured him that I was doing okay but just amazed by the atmosphere.

"Usually, at any given time, you'll see a topless woman walking around with barely anything on or nothing on at all. All I can tell you is to be prepared for the unexpected."

I took a quick glance over my shoulder and I began to shake my legs that were crossed at the knee. Dante' told me to be cool and reminded me that he would be by my side, no matter what. Just as he said that, the promoter of the club came over to the table and told Dante' that it was time to announce his latest rap group for their feature performance. He let him know that he'd be right there and to give him a few minutes. The promoter nodded then headed backstage as the lights began to dim.

Dante' signaled to one of the massive bouncers to come over to the table.

"This is a special lady who I want you to keep an eye on and make sure that she wants for nothing," Dante' said. I don't want a hair on her head out of place, you dig?"

"Not a problem," the bouncer stated to Dante' while looking in my direction.

"I have my cell phone on full blast so, in the event anything goes down or that you're uncomfortable with, don't hesitate to call me," he said to me. "I shouldn't be gone for more that fifteen minutes give or take a few. If you're hungry, let our servers know and they'll bring you something over to eat from the kitchen."

"I'm a little nervous but I'm sure with my new-found friend behind me, it's all good," as I nervously laughed out loud.

"Are you sure that you're going to be all right? If not, I can have someone else try to fill in for me."

"I'll be just fine Dante'. Go on so you can get back as soon as you can."

He gave me a kiss on the check and headed in the direction of the stage.

'I'm just playing along until all this blows over.'

The bouncer, whose name I found out later was Earl, asked me if I needed anything. I answered no, that I was good. He then stood to the side to let a few patrons by and sat to the left of me on his watch.

Several minutes later, the lights dimmed to almost black and a spotlight hit center stage. All of a sudden, a loud boom from the speakers that were located throughout the club ceiling and walls vibrated the floor around me. I jumped and moved closer to Earl the bouncer and he reassured me with a nod of his head that everything was all right. I exhaled several sighs of relief and then turned my attention back to the stage.

Shortly after, the DJ began to spin a hip hop mix of Montell Jordon's "This is How We Do it." The crowd went wild and jumped up from their seats as the strobe lights began to circle the stage and the crowd. The curtains opened from both sides and Dante' emerged. He was in a cream-colored pants suit that was opened at the chest to display his smooth caramel chest. He was blinged out from head to toe and, for a brief moment, I was caught up in his rapture and how fine he was. His whole persona was drenched in confidence and he knew that he owned the stage at that very moment. I took a number of gulps from my drink to calm my nerves and to cool the fire that was trying to get started in the back of my mind.

'Concentrate Brooke! You got it going on, girl— happiness is on the way back home, soon.'

I glanced around the club and saw how the women were going completely mad at the sight of Dante'. He was widely known in the music industry and I could only imagine how many women would love for him to take them home with him that night.

He had skills and knew how to wow the crowd, confidently, without being nervous or fazed by the groupies. After a short while, Dante' raised the microphone to his mouth to speak.

"Are you ready for the time of your life and to be entertained?"

The crowd yelled and clapped in approval.

"Can I get a hell yeah?" he said, while getting his swagger on. The crowd responded to his request.

"Can I get a hell yeah?" he said once again.

"All right, people, for those who don't know me, I'm the CEO of Blazin' Records. My name is Dante' Hunter, better known as Deuce-Deuce."

The crowd went wild again at the mention of his name.

"I'll be your MC for the first half of the show and will be introducing my hottest R&B group, Crave, that consists of three beautiful ladies straight from Atlanta. Carelle, Simone and Alexandria will sing to your heart's desire. Fellas, and maybe a few ladies out there, you won't be disappointed."

The crowd began to yell, clap and whistle after his last remark.

"Before they come out, I'd like to introduce Raw and Back Breaka. They make up the rap group, 'Annihilate.' Put your hands together! These brothas are about to tear it up and do the damn thing.

"Ladies and gentlemen without further ado, I give you, Annihilate!"

The DJ began to spin the group's music and the two members along with their posse took the stage. While the group performed, Dante' came out to check on me and let me know that he had a few more acts to announce and that he would be finished afterwards. He asked if I noticed anything that I would find unusual and then I gave him a look that said 'You've got to be kidding me.'

He saw the look on my face and laughed.

"You know what I mean, baby girl, do you recognize anyone or notice someone staring at you more than the norm?"

"No, not really. I still haven't gotten used to the idea of scantily-clad women and men parading throughout the club. I could have sworn I saw a blond-haired sister who resembled Lil Kim walk by me with nothing but a g-string on."

"I saw her walk pass me as I was coming to the VIP section. She was probably scoping out her latest booty call for the night. As the night goes on, and the more drinks that are consumed, you'll notice people becoming less inhibited and, at that point, all bets are off."

"I don't know how much more of this that I can stomach. Earl, over there, is keeping the danger at bay. I know that he won't let anything happen to me, but this is all way too uncomfortable to me and not my cup of tea, whatsoever."

"I know, baby girl, I promise that I won't be much longer and will get you out of here as quickly as possible."

He touched my back and gave me a reassuring rub and told me that he would be back in a few. I watched him step back onstage and then focused my attention to see if I knew any familiar faces.

Shortly after, Dante' appeared onstage to introduce the final act of the first part of the show. He announced that the segment of the show was to crown Ms. Nude Swinger of the Year. He stated that several women had been pre-selected and only four had made it to the finals.

"The qualifications to be crowned Ms. Nude Swinger of the Year is that the participant be an active member of the club, have the majority of the casting votes that were submitted via-email responses and, last but not least, have a slammin' body. We ask that our ladies take center stage."

The DJ played one of Lil Jon's rap hits and each contestant entered in barely-there bikinis and matching feathered masks covering their faces. To distinguish who was who, each of the women wore individual numbers attached to their bikini bottoms. The club owner then took the stage and Dante' handed over the microphone to him. The owner introduced each contestant by number to come forward and say a little something about themselves. After that, they took off their bikini tops to reveal their assets. It was obvious that many of them had breast enlargements and a few may have had some work done on their butts. Since I was sitting close to the stage, I was able to get a bird's eye view of everything. As the last contestant approached the microphone, she looked over in my direction. I hadn't paid much attention to the mocha-colored sister before now and realized that she looked very familiar. Dante' was standing off to the side of the owner of the club and also had a puzzled look on his face.

She began to tell the crowd why she should be chosen for Ms. Nude Swinger and spoke of her qualifications. She then took off her mask just as I was taking a sip of my drink and revealed her identity.

I began to choke and spit most of my drink on Earl who had a look of alarm on his face and reached for the inside of his jacket and then eagerly went into protective mode. I told him that I was okay and looked over towards the stage at the woman who stood before the crowd. She had her hands on her hips and then confidently turned her back to reveal her thong bikini bottom. She then untied the strings to her top and faced the crowd and looked over in my direction once again and smiled. The crowd cheered wildly because the woman was working her model shape and all of her assets to her favor. She knew that she had won the crowd over and that she might very well prevail and become the winner.

Before taking her place by the other contestants, she moved towards Dante' and stood before him and kissed him directly in the mouth. He was still in shock and didn't move an inch until the woman grabbed for his crotch and gave it a quick pinch. He yelped like a puppy that had his tail stepped on and then took several steps backwards. People started to laugh at his reaction and, for the first time since I met Dante', he looked completely embarrassed and humiliated.

He quickly regained his composure and gave a shaky laugh and pretended to brush it off. Dante' then made a comment about how frisky the cat was after chasing the mouse. This made the crowd laugh once again and I knew that Dante' was trying to keep face. A fine Italian shirtless man came over to where the announcer was and handed him the envelope with the contest results. The women whistled and gave their approval after he flexed his chest muscles and headed back stage.

The announcer opened the envelope then silently read the results before clearing his throat.

"Ladies and gentlemen it's time to name the runner up. With forty-seven percent of the votes the runner up is contestant number three, LeMonica Williams!"

LeMonica took several steps forward as she was crowned and given a sash naming her runner up.

"With fifty-three percent of the votes and, a well-known Gold member of the Swinger's Club, I announce your winner:

Gabrielle St. John. Gabrielle is better known as Gabby, to me, and her closest friends."

Gabby proudly took her reign as Ms. Nude Swinger of the Year. She was crowned and her sash was placed around her. She then strutted down the catwalk and stood directly before me and blew me a kiss. For the life of me, I couldn't move an inch—not even when Dante' sat beside me and asked was I okay. He called my name twice more before I could answer a weak yes with a slight nod of my head.

So, Gabby, my best friend since childhood, was the one who sent me the invitation to the Swinger's Ball.

" 'Well known member?' Did my ears hear correctly?'

She never let on that she was into anything remotely like a Swinger's Club. I know that we really didn't talk as much with one another for about a year while she traveled abroad.

'You never know people.'

I swallowed my entire drink without spitting it out and asked Dante' if could he get me another one. Before he could respond, I asked him what was up with Gabby grabbing his crotch and planting a fat kiss on him.

"We need to talk, Brooke," he said. "Let's blow this joint and head to my place and I'll explain everything."

He leaned over and said something to Earl and, after a nod of his head, Earl was off towards the entrance of the club.

"Let's go," he said. "The car should be waiting by the time we arrive outside."

I wanted nothing else but to shake Gabby by her curly mane and ask her why the hell was she practically nude on a stage in front a room full of horny people who were about to really get the party started in a couple of hours. She was surrounded by a group of people so I would save the Q&A for a later date. Dante' held the door open for me and I took one last glance at the stranger who masqueraded herself as my closet friend who never kept secrets from me.

"Boy do I feel like the fool." I said and Dante' led me to his awaiting car.

Chapter Twenty
When Players Play

We drove mainly in silence to Dante's condo until his cell phone rang. He looked at the caller I.D., grimaced then pushed the "End" button. I didn't even bother asking who was calling because I already knew. He asked me for the hundredth time was I all right and I told him that I was fine but wanted answers. Five minutes later, we drove to the private entrance of the parking garage and Dante' hit the gate button to let us in.

We pulled alongside his others vehicles and he let me out. Once again, his phone rang and he hit the "End" button. He turned his phone completely off after that and directed his full attention towards me.

I was still a little shaken, so he placed his arm around my waist and led me to the elevators. Once we arrived inside of his condo, he led me to the living room couch and asked if I wanted anything to drink. I knew alcohol was not something I needed right now because I wanted my head clear and my thoughts free to ask exactly what I needed to know. I told Dante' that a glass of iced water would be fine. He went behind the counter and pulled a glass from the cabinet and filled it with ice, grabbed a bottled water from the refrigerator and poured my water into the glass for me. He then sat directly beside me and clasped both his hands together and let out a long sigh.

"I'll start off by saying that I'm sorry that you had to witness the three-ring circus that happened on stage tonight. That was totally unplanned and I am pissed that it happened."

"First off, Dante', how do you know Gabby? It's obvious that you two know each other quite well and not just in passing. You two *seem* quite familiar with one another and, judging by the way she grabbed your crotch, I think you're acquaintances on a sexual level."

"You're completely right about all of it. Gabby was the fiancée who I was engaged to that I told you about," he said.

"The crazy deranged mad stalker is Gabby?" I blurted out before I knew it.

"Well yes, she's one in the same. I had no idea that she was a member of the Swinger's Club. She knew that I had promoted several of my upcoming groups and had even accompanied me to a few of them on several occasions. I never thought in a million years that she was a member but, looking back now, she had expressed interest in some of the events that were planned during this year."

We both acknowledged that she was the culprit behind the invitation, but what was her agenda?

"Do you think she knew that you and I had been seeing one another and had us followed?" I asked.

All of a sudden, everything hit me like a ton of bricks. The strange phone calls, the person outside of my window who tried to break into my home, and countless other events that seemed strangely out of place. I got angry and enraged with the entire situation. I then stood up and start pacing the floor. I kept asking myself aloud "Why? Why would Gabby do this to me when I thought we were the best of friends? Was she that hateful and jealous that she wanted to do harm to me?"

All Dante' could say was he didn't know. I knew that he had no idea that Gabby and I were best friends, but that still didn't keep me from directing my anger towards him, too.

I threw the glass to the floor, which startled Dante' and he jumped. He stood up with a concerned look on his face and attempted to hug me. I snatched back and told him not to touch me.

"How could you have kept your ex-fiancée's identity from me? I hate to be kept in the dark and, as a result, look what happened," I said.

I grabbed my purse from the couch and walked to the front door.

"Brooke, wait. Please don't leave like this. I had no idea that you and Gabby were best friends, let alone, knew each other. I tried to distance myself as far as I could away from her and, until recently, I thought I was doing a good job of it."

Deep down inside I knew that he was right and none of this was his fault. I couldn't breathe because I was so angry. I had to get away and get some fresh air to think. I opened the door and walked into the short hallway to the elevator and jabbed the down button a few times. Dante' was right on my heels trying to keep me from leaving in such a hurry and in a mess.

"Look, Brooke, I have an extra bedroom and you can stay until you cool down and I will take you home in the morning. I promise I won't bother you."

I knew that he was a man of his word but, after recent events, I wanted time alone to think and gather myself.

"I appreciate the offer Dante', but I need to be at home. I cannot believe all that has occurred tonight and I need time to be alone."

"At least let me take you home and make sure that you arrive safely," he insisted. "It's the least that I can do."

"That's unnecessary; I'll call a cab."

I could tell that I hurt his feelings but he relented, and insisted that he wait with me in the lobby until the cab arrived.

We both rode down in silence and took a seat in the lobby's reception area until the cab arrived five minutes later.

"Please call me and let me know that you made it home safely, and be sure to lock up after yourself."

I touched his shoulder to let him know that I would be all right and apologized for getting angry with him and gave him a hug and a kiss on the cheek. He closed the door once I got settled in the cab. I waved goodbye and gave the cab driver my address to my home. I then looked back and saw that Dante' was still standing outside. He remained in my sight until the cab driver turned the corner and drove in the direction to my home. If I knew that I wouldn't see him again, I would have hugged him for a few moments longer.

Chapter Twenty-One
No Stone Unturned

I arrived home shortly after one in the morning and attempted to pay my fare when the cab driver stated that the gentleman had already taken care of everything including the tip. I wasn't shocked and knew that Dante' genuinely cared, and perhaps, loved me. The cab driver said that he was expected to wait until I was in my house and to have me flip my porch light off and on to signal that I was securely locked in. I rummaged through my purse and found my keys, then told him, "Thank you," and wished him a good evening. After making it into my home, I closed and locked the door behind me, then flipped my porch light off and on twice and looked out the window as the cab was pulling away from the curb.

All of a sudden, I had the urge to get into the shower in an effort to cleanse away the night. I quickly walked to my room while discarding my shoes and dress along the way. I didn't even bother tying my hair back because I planned to wash it, too. After undressing, and while completely naked, I turned on the shower as hot as I could stand it. I stepped under the showerhead and let the water drench my entire body. I felt my tensed muscles loosen and grabbed my cucumber body wash to lather my body. After numerous washes, I shampooed and conditioned my hair. I quickly stepped from the shower and dried my body off with one of my plush bath towels and, after that, wrapped it around my body.

The shower helped relax my body but not my mind. I couldn't believe that Gabby failed to tell me anything about her relationship with Dante'. I was under the impression that she broke off her upcoming wedding because she wasn't ready to settle down and wanted to be focused on her career. Little did I know that she was the perfect liar and deceiver who masqueraded as an upstanding goal-oriented woman who had her life and career on track. As far as our friendship was concerned, it was over.

If she could do what she had done to others, and me, what else could she possibly be capable of doing?

For her own sake, I hoped she didn't attempt to contact me for whatever her sick reasons may have been. The girl had some issues that required a visit to the local psychiatrist.

'Oh yeah, medicating her crazy ass couldn't hurt either!'

I reached for my Palm Pilot to jot down a reminder to contact the detective assigned to my case and fill him in with the recent events that transpired. After I finished adding notes, I placed it on my night table, finished towel drying my hair and pulled a silk nightgown over my head then readied myself for bed.

I saw the caller I.D. light blinking on my home phone signaling that I had a message. I forgot to call Dante' and let him know that I was fine but I was sure that the cabby had already done so since he was tipped well from Dante'. I get the cordless phone and pushed the button for my voicemail. The automated voice said that I had two new messages.

"Hey, baby girl, I was just calling to make sure that you're all right. The cabby called me to let me know that you had made it in and signaled to him that everything was okay. I hope that you can accept my apologies for tonight's events and give me the chance to make it up to you soon. I'll give whatever time and space that you'll need, just call me when you can to let me know how you are getting along.

"You are a very special woman and none other like you exist. I truly love and care for you and only want your best interest put first. Well, I'm going to call it a night and I will talk with you soon. Good night baby girl, I love you."

I stared into space for several seconds as a lonely tear fell from my eye and sighed out of pure exhaustion. That man had a way with words and, for a brief moment, there was a thought of regret. I knew that I had made the better decision in choosing Myles.

I saved that message and went on to the next one that was left while I was in the shower. The last message was from Gabby.

"Hey girl, I was calling to see why you left so soon. I had hoped that you were having a blast. The look of shock and disbelief on you and Dante's faces were priceless. I told him that he couldn't get rid of me that easily and that I would make him pay for how he humiliated me and dumped me like two-day old garbage.

"Oh, I'm not done by far and if I were you, Brooke, I'd watch what company I keep, because in the long-run it might be deemed bad for your health. I think I will enjoy making you pay for stealing my man behind my back. And to think I let your overweight, pitiful, low self-esteem having, can't-get-a-man-to-save-her-own-life-and-keep-him chick be my friend. I did *you* a favor out of a debt and not kindness. So do us both a favor and just disappear, Bitch!" She abruptly snapped and ended the conversation after she released a burst of laughter in the phone.

I couldn't believe what my ears were hearing. I tried to recall what I did wrong in life to deserve this and, thus far, I could not think of a damned thing. All I knew was that Gabby wasn't playing with a full deck of cards and I was sure that her elevator stopped on three instead of going all the way to the twelfth floor.

I couldn't take anymore and collapsed into my bed pulling back the comforters. I was so tired and despondent that sleep overcame me in one quick wave. I had horrible dreams that Gabby was after me with a long, sharp sword. Just as she was about to strike, my dreams would start over with a new episode. The last dream I had was of Gabby holding me down on some sort of sacrificial table and repeatedly choking me and cutting me along my legs and hands with a twelve-inch butcher's knife. The pain was so real that I was sweating. The sweat trickled down my thighs and legs as I was struggling to sleep.

I finally forced myself awake and then realized that the sweat running down my legs and thighs weren't what I thought. It turned out to be blood.

I jumped to a sitting position but was knocked back by a blunt force to my chest. My bedroom walls began to zoom in and out and I had to struggle to remain focused and alert if I was to survive. When my vision cleared, I saw that the person was standing before me with a hunting knife and had tied my hands and feet together.

When speaking, the voice was filled with hate and venom directed only towards me.

"You think that you could take what is mine and get away with it? After all the hard work that I put into making my life? What—did you really think that a meager, weak woman such as yourself could take my livelihood away from me?" the intruder asked.

I was cut along my right check with the hunting knife and could feel my warm blood flowing down my cheek and drip onto my nightgown. The cut stung badly and I moaned in pain.

"I told you that I would make you pay and that's what I intend to do tonight, Bitch! I want your life for what you've done to me and make sure that you will never interfere in anyone else's business ever again—you're going down in the worst fashion!"

Even though my intruder was masked and clothed in black, I could never mistake who the voice belonged to. Over the many years, I had become familiar with it and could point out that person in a crowd of people by their voice alone. I, then, was violently yanked from my bed by the neck of my gown, thrown to my floor and scraped my knees on my broken cell phone that was discarded to prevent me from calling out for help. I was kicked in my right side along with being punched in the face where, minutes ago, I had been slashed. I couldn't believe that this was how I was going to die—by the hand of the person who hated me the most on earth but who I had done nothing wrong to.

"Before I end your miserable life, I want you to look me in the eye and beg for your life like the pig that you are." My assailant removed the mask and stood up in front of me while yanking me to my feet.

My guess was right all along. I could point out Roger Billings from his voice without looking at him and be right on the money.

"You stupid, bitch. You thought that you could go over my head repeatedly and snitch on me in order to get me fired. I worked my ass to the tailbone for that job for over twenty years and not once did I get the recognition that I deserved! I cannot count the many hours spent trying to prove myself and then to have a fat trollop like you outshine me each and every chance you got.

"You humiliated me for the very last time a couple of weeks ago. I complained about you and I was let go from my position! How is a man of my age supposed to start over again? No one wants a middle-aged man like me when there's a young, eager-eyed college student willing to do what I do for half the pay. There's no way that I can start all over again at entry-level pay. As a result of your interfering, I lost my wife, and my home because of you and now it's time that you pay the price!"

I was gagged with electrical tape and couldn't scream when I saw him raise his knife and plunge it into my abdomen not once, but twice.

"Lord Jesus!" I screamed through the tape that masked my cries to my heavenly father. I fell to my knees and collapsed to the floor.

"And just so you know, I took care of your big boy rapper friend Pilate or Picante for making a fool out of me that day along the expressway when I accidentally hit the back of his truck. Yeah Bitch, that was me! I've been following you both for some time now and watched your every move. So tonight, I killed two birds with one stone!" he said while he laughed at his own dry sense of humor.

My breathing became labored and I could see all my blood pooling around me on the floor. From a distance I could hear my front door open and slam shut as Mr. Billings left my home. I could see that the contents of my purse had been tossed to the floor along with my shattered cell phone. I spotted my car keys lying on the floor next to my purse and mustered enough strength to grab them and find the panic button on my alarm that I used to set my home when I left.

"Lord, if it be your will to live, please allow me my day of justice! Please allow me to hear, 'Effective Immediately, Roger Billings, you are ordered to serve life in prison without parole. Also, I guess this will tell if it's meant for Myles and I to marry. Thank you Jesus. Thank you for all you have done, and, yes, I accept you as my one and only savior for life. I always have!"

I suddenly felt cold as everything faded to black and my breathing became labored. I closed my eyes and let the waves of darkness overcome me with the alarm button still in my bloody hands.

"Will anyone come for me? Did the alarm really go off? Will I make it to become Myles' wife? Oh Jesus—can't breathe. The, the room is spinning. I, I—"

www.ingramcontent.com/pod-product-compliance
Lightning Source LLC
Chambersburg PA
CBHW070601180626
46817CB00005B/1938